MW01139736

Broken Branches

Other books by Brenda M. Spalding

The Alligator Dance

The Green Lady Inn Mystery Series

Broken Branches
Whispers in Time
Hidden Assets
The Spell Box

Blood Orange
Honey Tree Farm – for the Love of the Beekeeper's
Daughter
Bottle Alley

A Murder for Christmas
(short story)

Brenda M Spalding

Broken Branches

THE GREEN LADY INN
BOOK 1

Written by
Award-winning author

Brenda M. Spalding

Copyright

Copyright © 2014 Brenda M. Spalding
ISBN 978-1-5394-071-6-4

All rights reserved

No part of this publication may be reproduced, stored in a
retrieval system, transmitted in any form or by any means,
electronic, mechanical, photocopying, recording, or
otherwise, without prior written permission of the
publisher, the author, or her heirs.

Published by:
Heritage Publishing. US
www.heritagetpublishingus.com

Brenda M Spalding

For my Father,
Ambrose Farrell,
Who always believed in me.
He showed me how to see beyond my world,
and to appreciate my Irish Heritage.

Broken Branches

Brenda M Spalding

The Claddagh Ring

The Claddagh Ring history dates back over 300 years to a small fishing village in Ireland near Galway called Claddagh. It was here the tradition of the Claddagh rings first started.

Claddagh comes from the Irish term 'An Cladach' that means a 'flat stony shore.' This was a pretty and ancient village with winding streets and small thatched-roofed mud houses.

The First Theory

Margaret Joyce inherited a vast amount of money from her late husband named Domingo de Rona. He was a wealthy Spanish merchant trading with Galway in Ireland. She later married the Mayor of Galway (Oliver Og French) in 1596 and used her inherited wealth to construct many bridges in Connacht. The first Claddagh ring was supposed to be her providential reward.

The Second Theory

A native of Galway by the name of Richard Joyce was captured by the Algerians and sold as a slave to a Moorish goldsmith. Later—in 1689—William III of England demanded the release of all British subjects. Richard Joyce was released from slavery as well. The goldsmith then offered Richard Joyce a significant portion of his wealth and his only daughter in marriage if he would agree to stay in Algiers. Richard Joyce refused all the tempting offers, returning to Galway with the first Claddagh ring.

Brenda M Spalding

Chapter 1

"Okay, Gran, I promise. I'll come up to Salem this weekend for sure," Megan said, perched on the corner of her mother's old antique desk, her long legs dangling over the side.

She glanced at her calendar and thought about all she had to arrange for her art gallery to function in her absence. Her assistants were great; she just had to make sure they knew what needed to be done. After all, it was only for a weekend. Today was Tuesday the fifteenth—the ides of October. She frowned, hoping that wasn't a bad omen. No, there was plenty of time to get things organized.

Megan had a growing reputation as a brilliant watercolorist and held painting classes in the back studio. Her classes were always full, but there were no classes on the weekends.

"Sorry to have to cut this short, Gran, but I have a lot to do if I'm going to take time off for a visit. I love you," she said.

"Yes, dear, I know how busy you are with your gallery. But I've got to talk to you about something. It really can't wait any longer. I'm not getting any younger, and there are things you need to know. I need your help, and I'd rather just…" Gran's voice trailed off.

"Gran, are you there?"

Megan's grandmother whispered into the phone, "I heard something upstairs just now." Lately, she'd heard a lot of strange sounds in the old house that had been in her family for generations. "Sorry. I thought I heard something again."

"What do you mean, 'again'? Gran, what did you hear?"

"Got to go! See you soon!"

Megan stared at the unresponsive phone in her hand. "What the hell was that all about?" she shrugged.

After a little while, Megan called her grandmother back but got no answer. Megan was a bit concerned but knew Gran had friends she often went out with. She would try and call again later.

"Now for these invoices, or I'm not going anywhere. I do need to hire a bookkeeper," Megan said. She busied herself with paperwork and the gallery for the rest of the day. In between, she looked up flights from New York to Boston, checking times and prices. All the while, disturbing questions about her grandmother and the strange ending of their conversation invaded her thoughts.

*****

Megan's grandmother hung up the phone and stood there, waiting to see if the sounds she heard would repeat.

"I must be losing it for real," she said aloud, talking to herself.

Then she heard it again, a noise like furniture being dragged across the floor. Quietly and as quickly as she could manage, she pulled herself up the stairs by the handrail. She stopped on the landing to catch her breath and listened. She hadn't been upstairs in the last few years. There it was again, above her, coming from the attic.

She walked down the hallway and eased open the door leading up to the attic. She was positive someone was up there. She decided to go and call the police. As she turned, her foot caught on the carpet, and she bumped her elbow hard on the door frame, sending a painful zing up her arm.

"Ow! Damn, that hurt," she whispered, hoping her stifled exclamation hadn't been heard in the attic. She held her breath, praying to be able to get away before being seen. As she shuffled down the hall, she heard someone rush down from the attic. She made it only to the top of the stairs when she felt a hand grip her shoulder and shove her hard.

The answer to Megan's unanswered questions came the next morning when a Salem police officer called to inform her that Corey Elizabeth Bishop, Megan's grandmother, had been found dead at the bottom of her stairs.

Chapter 2

Megan's assistant, Jennifer, knocked on Megan's office door. She walked in and found her boss sitting behind her desk, crying. "Megan, what's wrong?" she asked.

"That call was from the Salem police in Massachusetts. My grandmother is dead! I can't believe it. I just talked to her yesterday and was planning to visit her. I haven't been up in a while," Megan choked out between sobs while wiping her tears. "I knew she was getting on, but I didn't think she was that bad."

Megan took a deep breath. "Jen, I'm going to have to take some time off to deal with this. I have to go to Salem. Oh, God, Jen, how do people do this? I can't even think straight right now."

"Don't worry about the gallery. You go and take care of things up there, and we'll take care of things here. Annie can handle the invoices. The current exhibition will be up for a few more weeks, and by then, you should be back. You have a good team here, and we can reach you by phone if we have questions." Jennifer handed Megan more tissues, helped her with her coat, and walked her out.

On her way home on the subway, Megan recalled all the wonderful times she'd had at her gran's house. As a child, she had spent a couple of weeks there every summer. She and Gran walked the beach looking for the best shells to decorate the towering sand castles they built together.

Recalling those summers brought her parents to mind. Years ago, they had been killed by a drunk driver. A Sunday trip to the Hamptons to check out a new gallery had made Megan an orphan.

Back at her apartment, Megan flopped down in a chair and cried again softly. The shock of the news was wearing off. She started making mental notes of all she needed to arrange.

She spent the afternoon on her computer, looking up funeral homes in Salem. She chose one and called them. The funeral director was wonderful and said he would take care of most of the details. Then she called Delta and booked a flight to Boston for the next day.

*****

"Damn peepers!" Megan screamed.

Once again, she had to swing around another slow-moving vehicle on Route 107 out of Boston. Why in heaven's name they weren't on Route 9, or better yet, out in the Berkshires, she didn't know. She had to admit, though, that the fall colors were beautiful to see. All the shades of red from burgundy to crimson, yellow amber to canary, tangerine oranges, and browns mixed up in a rich fall palette brushed through the trees of the New England countryside. The trees wore their party dresses, and the guests were arriving by carload and busload. It was the middle of October. The lazy days of summer were over, and a crisp chill was in the air. Before long, the trees would be bare and snow on its way.

Memories of childhood days came flooding back, going to the Clam Box in Ipswich, standing in line with Gran outside the bright red-and-white striped building, patiently waiting their turn. That had been one of Gran's favorite restaurants, and she tried to get there several times each year, especially in the fall, before the restaurant closed for the winter. The last time Megan had visited, she took Gran there. Megan tried to visit as often as she could, but recently life kept getting in the way.

She had so many recollections of time spent with her grandmother. Gran always treated her to real maple syrup in tin cans with old-fashioned scenes of maple harvesting and maple sugar candy in the shape of maple leaves. She turned apples from the local orchards into delicious pies. Autumn in New England was undoubtedly a magical time. Even the air smelled different.

As she drove past the "Welcome to Salem" sign, another fond tradition came to mind: Pumpkin Sunday. The Sunday before Halloween, her parents would pick up Gran early and drive into the country and look at a hundred pumpkins before deciding on the perfect one. Back at Gran's, they would spread newspapers on the kitchen table and carve that pumpkin into a jack-o'-lantern masterpiece.

Gran was always so much fun to be with. Megan was going to miss her very much. Her eyes blurred with tears. Maybe someday I'll have children of my own to share Pumpkin Sunday with, she mused. She would tell them about her gran and how wonderful she was. Right now, she just wished the damn leaf peepers would get out of her way and let her get to the house before nightfall. Her early morning flight from New York had been on time, and she had picked up her rental car and was on her way without any hiccups—except for the dawdling rubbernecks.

She didn't drive much, living in New York, and was out of practice. It felt strange to be driving, and the extra traffic didn't help.

She was very anxious to get to Gran's house and contact Thompson's Funeral Home—"Compassion in Your Time of Need"—and check on the plans she had made before she left New York. The internet was great when you had to find a funeral home and a church on short notice.

Route 107 from Boston to Salem was a road she knew well. Sixteen miles and a half-hour drive were all it took. She had gone to Salem many times with her family. Her mom, Mary, had grown up in Salem. She went to school at the Massachusetts College of Art and Design in Boston, where she had met and married Megan's dad, Peter Calloway. When Mary and Peter graduated, they had started a quaint art gallery in Greenwich Village.

Megan had attended the New York Academy of Art and settled in New York City, helping her parents run the gallery. After they died, the small but successful business became hers, and she adored it.

Megan gained a good reputation as a talented watercolor artist, and her gallery was creating a buzz for exhibiting up-and-coming new artists. She loved the art scene in New

York. Mixing with other artists and attending gallery openings with friends was great. The arts and culture were a big part of Megan's life in the city. She couldn't imagine doing anything else.

She was also a very attractive woman. Shoulder-length, dark-chestnut hair flecked with gold highlights enhanced her unusual green eyes. Her daily runs in Washington Square Park kept her figure neat and trim, just adding to the package.

Many a man fell for her beauty, brains, and talent. She'd had some relationships, but nothing had ever become serious for her. She always felt that something was missing. She had never been able to make that connection with anyone she dated. She had found each too insecure or too involved with himself—and not with her. She was not a trophy to dangle on any man's arm.

Now her beloved grandmother was gone. But not before saying she had something to talk over with Megan and wanted her advice. Gran had never asked for help with anything before. That alone worried Megan. The whole conversation had made her anxious about what was going on with her grandmother.

Megan was coming to visit, just not the way Gran had in mind. The funeral was on Saturday, with the wake on Friday. The funeral home assured her they would take care of things and put the obituary in the paper.

Megan liked going to wakes and funerals. An Irish wake was like a party, with all the friends and relatives, aunts and cousins, to visit and share stories about the poor deceased.

It was also a good chance to catch up and hear about all the happenings throughout the family. Who had gotten married? Who had gotten divorced? What college was some cousin attending? The whisperings: "Did you hear about so and so?" and finding out you were the only one who didn't know the secret.

There is nothing as grand as an Irish wake unless it's the reception after the funeral where the Irish whiskey flows and the food is piled high. Uncle Henry will tell his stories about the old country while all the cousins try to figure out who belongs to what branch of the family tree. They speculate on who is the next to go so they can get together again. Would it be Aunt Hattie? She's in her nineties. Could it be Cousin Fred? He's still smoking like a chimney and drinking like a fish. No one wishes anyone ill, but they all realize death comes to everybody in time.

Chapter 3

A few more minutes, a couple of turns, and Grandma Corey's house would be there, just like always, except this was not like always. Gran was not going to greet her with a great big hug, tea, and cookies. She remembered Gran's flowered tea pot with the chip on the spout and small matching cups and plates. Megan loved having a tea party with Gran.

Megan felt herself getting all misty again and gave herself a mental shake. She would not break down and cry, not now or at the wake or the funeral. Gran would say to suck it up and get on with it. Besides, Gran loved a good wake and funeral, too. It just so happened that at this one, Gran would be the guest of honor.

Finally, at the last turn, there was the house standing in front of her. Megan pulled into the driveway, shut off the engine, and just sat and stared at the old place. Megan loved how Gran kept the flowers blooming in the front yard through to Thanksgiving—chrysanthemums that matched the colors of the trees displayed around it. For the last couple of years, Gran had not planted and kept up with the garden as she had before. Gran had been slowing down. Megan had closed her eyes over the past few years to how much her grandmother was aging.

Soon the trees would be shedding all their colorful leaves of fall, and the yard would need raking. What fun she'd had as a kid jumping in those piles of crunchy leaves.

She also remembered the Christmas visits, seeing decorative poinsettias on the porch, and playing in the snow with the neighborhood kids how she loved making snow angels! Gran always had some hot chocolate ready after the snowman was properly dressed in an old hat and scarf.

She imagined her grandmother at the door. Gran was a short, gray-haired woman, a bit on the heavy side, with glasses perched on her nose. Gran was always shoving the glasses back in place when they slipped down her nose, which they did a lot.

She often wore a house dress with a cobbler's apron over it. She had to have pockets and always had treats hidden in them. And Gran gave the very best big, squishy hugs.

Megan dug into her own pockets for some tissues; sure, she was going to cry again and struggling not to. The memories were happy ones, but she was sad at the same time.

She could see from the outside that the old house needed help—a lot of it. Megan wept a bit at seeing the state of the once beautiful manor.

The house, a federal design, was built in the early 1850s. A columned portico covered the brick entry steps. Some of those bricks had now crumbled or were missing. The shutters that accented the windows used to be emerald green. Now the paint was peeling, and some of the shutters were in danger of falling off completely. The original cedar board slats showed through the dingy, cracked, white paint.

Next to the house was a garage that, at one time, had been the carriage house with stalls for horses. It had a small room over it that had not been used for many years. It was probably the groom's quarters—back when there was a need for one. She had no idea what might be up there now.

Megan blamed herself for not keeping in touch more often with her grandmother and not taking the time to come up and visit. Her infrequent visits were not enough. Her grandmother had seemed quite healthy in mind and body for someone who was eighty-three. Gran always sounded so in control, but now Megan saw she hadn't been. She should have done more. The old Irish guilt overwhelmed her again, and Megan broke her promise to herself not to cry.

Chapter 4

"Okay, enough self-pity," Megan said out loud, using the damp tissue to dry her eyes.

She needed to get herself going to make the house presentable for visitors after the burial. Megan had only a little time to get things in order, so she looked up local caterers online, called several, and hired one to provide the food.

She fished out the spare key her grandmother had given her a while back. Megan never thought she would need it, but Gran had said take it, "just in case." The key turned in the lock. Megan pushed open the heavy oak door and stepped into memories of her childhood.

The light spilled in to reveal the familiar, large foyer with its black and white tiles. Straight ahead, a large, round, mahogany table holding a crystal vase with dusty, dried flowers sat under a sweeping, curved staircase. To the right of the grand staircase was the dining room. A hallway led from the front door past the bottom of the stairs to the back of the house where the kitchen was. The kitchen originally had been a separate building behind the house to keep the whole house from going up in flames in case of fire. A long-forgotten renovation had connected it to the main house.

On the left side of the hallway was a sitting room with a huge fireplace. The next room, the old library, had been used as the family room for as long as she could remember.

Other renovations had created a combination bedroom, sitting room, and bathroom suite behind the present kitchen. It looked like Gran had used it as her bedroom for quite a while.

When was the last time I was here? Megan struggled to remember. Was it a few months ago? No, that's wrong. It's been more like a year, she thought.

As Megan roamed from room to room on the bottom floor, she saw the signs of age.

There were worn and threadbare rugs, chips on the painted woodwork, and dust everywhere. The kitchen was the worst. The floor was sticky, dirty dishes were piled in the sink, and cooking grease caked the stove. Plus, it was a time warp back to the seventies, when it had last been remodeled. There were avocado appliances that had been the rage then but looked odd now. The kitchen table was chrome-framed with an aged, yellow Formica top. It had matching chairs whose cracked vinyl seats were mended with silver duct tape.

Oh, God, this will take an army to clean up, Megan thought. If I can just get the bottom floor in decent shape, it'll be okay.

She was tempted to consider getting a hotel room, but at this time of year, she wasn't sure she could with all the fall visitors in the area. She was near to tears again and wished her mom was around to guide her.

"This is ridiculous," she said aloud. "I can and will do this."

Megan looked up house cleaners on her smartphone and made some calls. After begging and pleading, she convinced a cleaning crew to come in the morning to get the house ready. She had no idea how many relatives and friends of Gran's would come, but she wanted to make her Grandma Corey proud.

She ordered Chrysanthemums in all the fall colors: a lovely spray for the casket, a beautiful centerpiece for the table by the front stairs, and two matching bouquets for the tables the caterer would use.

Her final call was to China Village, a local restaurant. They delivered an early dinner of mild Szechuan chicken, fried rice, and an eggroll in twenty minutes. Damn the calories tonight.

After her meal, she was too tired to deal with a hotel, so she carried her bags up the wide staircase. As she walked down the hall, she automatically closed the door leading to the attic. Had she heard something? She stopped and listened. No, it was just her imagination working overtime.

*****

She set her luggage in the room she had always chosen as a child. One of six large bedrooms on the second floor, this room had a view of the back gardens. The room was decorated in a delicate shell, pink and pristine white. She used to count the rosebuds on the wallpaper as a child before she fell asleep. She always felt like a princess in the big, antique, four-poster bed. Her gran would spray the scent of roses in the room for her every time she slept there.

The wallpaper was faded now and soiled with water damage around the window and one corner near the ceiling. Dust motes, streaming through the window and dancing in the late afternoon sun, showed how worn the faded carpet was. The room smelled quite musty from having been neglected for so long. She picked up a jar of shells she remembered collecting on her trips to the beach. She blew off the thick dust and coughed. The unspoiled fairy-tale bedroom was something else from her childhood that was only a memory now.

Megan folded back the dusty quilt and flopped on the bed. She wondered how much it would cost to get a chimneysweep in to put the fireplaces in working order again. She would need to have the large fireplace inspected if she decided to use it.

"What am I thinking? I'm only going to be here a few days," she said. "It's wake, funeral, reading of the will, and then back to New York. That's the plan, and I'm sticking to it."

However, the best-laid plans don't always work out the way they are supposed to. Soon Megan's objective of a quick getaway would be dramatically changed, as would be the rest of her life.

Chapter 5

The wake on Friday night at Thompson's Funeral Home
was very interesting, indeed. Megan anticipated maybe a
few people would show up to remember her grandmother.
What she didn't expect was how big a crowd did show up
to pay their last respects. It was standing room only, and
there were flowers everywhere. She didn't know her
grandmother was so well known and well-liked.

Mass cards and sympathy cards had been arriving at the
house, and there was another neat pile of them beside the
casket. A lot of people had donated to the Salem Historical
Society in Grandma Corey's name. Megan didn't even
realize that her grandmother had been interested in the
historical society. There was so much she didn't know
about her grandmother. She started to wonder if she had
known her at all. Gran was more than warm hugs and
chocolate-chip cookies.

Megan sat on an antique sofa to receive the visitors. Her
cousin Maureen had just left her when someone said, "Hi,
Megan. We haven't met, but I knew your grandmother."

Megan looked up to see a woman she thought might be
in her late seventies. She seemed out of place and not at all
like a mourner at a wake. The woman's hair was a shade of
red that even Lady Clairol could not conjure up. The
frames of her glasses were emerald green, and her lipstick
almost the same tint as her hair. The colors continued to her
clothes. A colorful wrap around her shoulders in an array of

emerald, gold, and rust matched the flowing, floor-length skirt and completed the outfit.

"May I sit for a bit?" the flamboyant person asked.

"Of course, thank you for coming," Megan said as she extended her hand.

"All your grandmother's friends are so glad to meet you, Megan. Your grandmother was very proud of you and your art and the gallery. I'm just so sorry about the circumstance. Corey was a lovely lady and a great friend to everyone she met. Oh, and my name is Clarissa McDowell. I work for the Salem Museum, and I'm a member of the historical society. I talked with your grandmother often about Salem and other things."

Her voice dropped to a whisper, and she motioned for Megan to come closer. "I need to talk to you in private. Some things were not right with your grandmother the last few years. She was losing her eyesight, for one thing. She used to joke that if she couldn't see the mess in her house, she could pretend it didn't exist. She was too stubborn and too proud to ask for help of any kind. I don't want to go into it here. I'll be at the funeral tomorrow, and maybe we can arrange to have a chat back at the house afterward. I definitely must speak to you before you head back to New York."

Clarissa patted Megan on the shoulder and stood, moving on to greet others attending the wake.

Well, that was a weird conversation, Mega thought. What was that all about? This whole thing just gets "curiouser and curiouser," to quote Alice.

Megan didn't have time to dwell on what Clarissa had said as more guests expressed their condolences. There were cousins and relatives she had not seen in years, and some she didn't recognize at all. The older ones shared tales about Corey in her younger years. By the time the wake was over, Megan was exhausted and just wanted to get back to the house and her bed.

Chapter 6

Megan arrived at her grandmother's house just after ten and let herself in. It had been a long and stressful evening. She stopped and looked back at the door. "I thought I locked that when I left. I must be more tired than I thought," she said.

She shook her head and went to the kitchen. The back door was ajar. "What the hell? I need to be more careful with the doors. I could swear I locked both before I left."

She opened the door and looked outside, down the porch, and across the garden.

She stepped out onto the porch and didn't see anyone hiding there or anything out of place that she could tell. The back porch was a dumping ground for a lot of gardening stuff from over the years. Old pots and seed trays, rusted garden shovels, and boxes of old seed packets were strewn from one end to the other.

The garden was dark, but nothing moved in the shadows that she could see. But someone was watching Megan check out the back porch. A figure dressed in black stood behind a large rhododendron at the back of the garden, thankful he had not been caught. Megan was not a half-blind old lady. He would have to be more careful in the future.

He tossed the house keys in his hand before putting them back in his pocket and crept away.

Chapter 7

On the day of the funeral, Megan woke up early, hurried with her shower, and made some coffee to get her started. The caterer was coming at nine, and she needed to be at the funeral home by ten to go over the details and meet the priest. She had let the funeral director choose the clergyman for the graveside service since she had no idea which church Gran had attended.

The caterers were busy setting up when the liquor store delivered the beer, wine, and the necessary Irish whiskey. The florist arrived with lovely bouquets of chrysanthemums in all the autumn hues for the entry foyer and the dining room table. Megan had chosen the same mix of colors for the casket spray. She would not let her grandmother go without a proper send-off. She had loved her grandmother and felt guilty for not being more involved in her life when she was here.

Megan was the only passenger in the limo that followed the hearse to the cemetery. The very long funeral procession held up traffic all over Salem as it wound its way to the cemetery. Megan was amazed that the quiet and gentle grandmother she remembered had touched so many lives.

The service was an eye-opener for her. The priest seemed to have known her grandmother and named all the organizations she had participated in over the years. She was the secretary for the woman's guild and treasurer of the garden club. She had also supported the Salem Historical Society and the local theater.

Megan saw Clarissa in the crowd of guests at the graveside and nodded to her. Clarissa's costume was a little more subdued this time. She wore a combination of royal purple, dark periwinkle, and black, and her deep-purple glasses matched her lipstick. Clarissa nodded back and put her finger to her lips, a signal to keep quiet.

Keep quiet about what? Megan thought.

Soon the service was over, and everyone was leaving. Megan lingered a few minutes longer.

"Gran," she said, "I'm so sorry I didn't keep in touch. I never thought you would die so suddenly like this, just like Mom and Dad. I always let my own life come first, thinking there would be time later, always later. Now there is no later, and I'm sorry. I hope I'm at least giving you a great good-bye. I already miss you." Megan wiped the tears from her eyes and asked, "Why were you on those stairs?"

By the time Megan was back at the house, the caterers were ready and had done a wonderful job. They had stacked lovely white china plates trimmed in silver at one end of the buffet table.

A bar was set up, with shining glassware that glittered in the sunlight streaming through windows that now were clean, thanks to the efforts of the cleaning crew she had hired. The whole place looked wonderful. Megan was sure Grandma Corey would have approved.

As the guests began arriving, she exchanged small talk with her relatives. Sometimes she had to pretend she knew who they were talking about. She realized that she had been out of contact with her family for way too long.

After a while, the guests started to leave. The caterers cleaned up, and only one half-finished bottle of Irish whiskey and a couple of bottles of wine remained.

Megan noticed that Clarissa had stayed behind and not left with the others. She sat on the end of the couch, waiting for her chance to have that private talk she had mentioned at the wake.

"Sorry, Megan, I know you probably think it a bit strange, my wanting to get you alone, but there are things you need to know. I hope you don't mind."

Clarissa patted the seat next to her for Megan to sit down. Instead, Megan took a chair across from Clarissa. She was not that trusting of this colorful visitor.

"First, my dear, I don't think Corey's fall was an accident. She told me she thought some-thing strange was going on in the house. Things were moved. Lamps she thought she had turned off were on. Lights she had left on would be off. It was nothing she could put her finger on. She started to think she was losing it.

"Corey was only in her eighties and still had all her marbles," she continued. "She felt that someone else was in the house. She believed in ghosts and thought maybe she had one. That was easier to accept than the thought that she was going cuckoo. She didn't want to end up in a home for crazies! But I swear she was being gaslighted—you know, being made to feel that she was losing her mind. Someone was trying to make her move out of the house."

Clarissa sniffled, took a tissue out of her purse, and dabbed her eyes. She tried not to make a fool out of herself. Megan waited for her to continue.

"There was a man, a Mr. Prendergast, who made Corey several offers on the house. He wants to turn it into condos. A lot of people commute from Salem to their jobs in Boston, you know. Many of the old houses have gone that way. Not much call for a big house with six bedrooms anymore." Clarissa blew her nose and continued.

"Corey wanted to ask you what she should do. I know you two haven't talked much lately, but you were the only close family she had since your mom died. Corey was afraid of what the future would bring. She wasn't ready for a home for the elderly but felt she might not have a choice. She wanted to stay in her home, and she was thinking of asking you to come and live with her in Salem, at least for a while until she decided what to do." Clarissa stopped talking and wiped her eyes again. She sighed deeply and looked at Megan.

"I don't know what to say," Megan answered, nervously kicking her foot, clearly distressed by the news. "This is so much to take in. And who is this, Mr. Prendergast, anyway?"

Before Clarissa could answer, Megan decided to trust her and hoped she was doing the right thing.

"Gran called me the morning she died and said she wanted to talk to me about something. I had no idea what it was about," Megan said. "And when I got home from the wake last night, the front door wasn't locked, and I know I locked it. And then, in the kitchen, the back door wasn't closed all the way, and I remember locking that, too. I thought maybe I had so much on my mind that I did forget to lock them, but now I'm wondering if maybe something is going on here."

"That's exactly the kind of thing that happened to Corey," said Clarissa. "Corey was very worried—and rightly so because now she's dead!" Clarissa sobbed a bit, struggled to compose herself, took a deep breath, and wiped her eyes again.

"Now, about Mr. Prendergast, he's a big wheeler-dealer in town, or at least he thinks he is. In my opinion, he's a pompous ass who thinks he's better than the rest of us. I'm sure he'll come crawling around as soon as the dust settles. He was at the wake but stayed in the back. He was checking you out. He might be okay, but I don't trust him."

Clarissa watched Megan try to stifle a yawn. "I really should go," she said. "You must be exhausted. You ought to rest and have a bit of time to yourself. But please, you take care. Come by the historical society any time you need to chat. I'm there most days."

Clarissa got up and grabbed her coat and purse. She hugged Megan, and together they walked to the front door.

"Don't worry too much about me," Megan said. "I'm a big-city girl, and I'll deal with Mr. Prendergast. The will is being read Monday when I see a Mr. Halloran. Grandma Corey might have left the house to the historical society or someone else. We'll wait and see. It might not be mine to sell."

"Well, at least I've warned you. I hope I see you soon, Megan. I'm glad I talked to you about all of this," Clarissa said as she walked down the front walkway and drove off in her dilapidated, old red Jeep. The car was as colorful as she was, with its dented fenders painted in whatever colors had been on hand when touch-ups were needed, which was often.

"Oh, Gran, what have you gotten me into?" Megan said to no one in particular as she walked back into the house and turned the lock on the door.

*****

Megan puttered around for the next couple of hours, cleaning up and looking through the kitchen cabinets and cupboards. No matter who got the house, she would have to clear out her grandmother's stuff, and there was a lot of it.

She sat down at the kitchen table and made a list of all she needed to do. First, she must locate all of Gran's important papers, and then she should gather anything useful for the Goodwill or Salvation Army. She also planned to call someone to appraise things she thought might be of value—such as her grandmother's lovely collection of crystal and china. Some of it was Waterford Crystal and seemed very old.

Another memory surfaced, of the family sitting around the dining room table, a beautiful flower arrangement in the center, surrounded by places set with all Gran's sparkling china and crystal. Megan didn't remember the occasion. It might have been a birthday or anniversary. She sighed.

Later she grabbed some leftover food out of the fridge and settled down in front of an ancient television to try and relax before heading up to bed. Her mind kept going over all that had happened the last couple of days—especially about the concerns that Clarissa had raised. She found it hard to keep her eyes open and nodded off.

Chapter 8

A knock at the door woke her up.

"Coming, coming!" she shouted, annoyed by the interruption of her rest. "I'm coming," she said as she got to the door.

"Hello! I hope we didn't disturb you. We live next door and knew your grandmother."

Megan looked questioningly at the two strangers, a man, and a woman, on her doorstep.

"We didn't know her well; we moved in only a few months ago," said the man, who looked to be about her age. "She was a nice lady, very welcoming, and she always took the time to stop and chat. Here's a container of pasta sauce and a box of spaghetti. Amanda makes the most fantastic pasta sauce. Figured you might get tired of leftover sandwiches and need something hot."

The two young people handed the offerings to Megan.

"I'm sorry. Who are you?" Megan asked, still groggy from her nap and not a little confused.

"Oh, sorry, I'm Zack Longstreet, and this is my wife, Amanda. We should have introduced ourselves. We have an art gallery in town, and Saturday is our busiest time. We couldn't come over until we closed the gallery for the day," Zack explained.

Megan perked up. "You have an art gallery? Really? I'm an artist in New York—a water-colorist actually—and I

have my own gallery. Pleased to meet you. Finally—
someone normal!"

"Well, I don't know about normal," said Amanda,
smiling. "Artists tend to be a bit quirky—in a good way."

"Where are my manners? Please come in," Megan said.
"Would you like something to drink, coffee, tea, wine? I've
got plenty."

"I'd love a glass of white wine if you have it," said
Amanda, taking a seat on the couch.

"Red for me, if you don't mind," said Zack, helping
himself to the seat beside Amanda.

"I'll be right back. I can't wait to hear all about your
gallery," said Megan as she headed for the kitchen. She
poured three glasses of wine, a good Malbec for Zack, and
a nice Pinot Grigio for Amanda and herself. Megan was
thrilled to have neighbors visit, especially since she didn't
know anyone in Salem.

Zack was of average height and a little on the thin side.
He took off his frayed, wide-brimmed, canvas hat that had
seen better days to reveal a very bald head. His hairless
head was at odds with his extremely full and long reddish-
brown beard. Despite the season, Zack was still wearing
shorts and sandals. They were covered with varying shades
of paint.

Amanda was lovely, small and dark-haired, with
beautiful, big brown eyes. Her hair curled its way around
her face and down her back, shimmering in the light.
Megan was already imagining painting her if Amanda

would agree. Maybe she would have time to do a sketch and paint it later when she got back to New York.

"Here you go," Megan said as she handed the glasses to her guests. "Now, tell me all about that gallery."

Over the next hour or so, Amanda, Zack and Megan got to know each other and discussed the small but interesting art culture in Salem. The gallery was close enough to Boston for clients to visit and far enough away to have lower rental rates.

"It's the best of both worlds," Zack said.

"We thought about going to the Cape, but there you get only the summer crowds, and the rates are high," said Amanda.

"We thought about Newton or Wellesley, but rental property is pretty expensive there, too," Amanda explained. "We got a great deal on a gallery here that went out of business. It even had an office and studio in the back and only needed a little cleaning out. It seemed like we were destined to have it."

After making Megan promise to visit the gallery before she left Salem, Amanda and Zack headed home. Megan was delighted and happy to have had someone to talk to about art and galleries. It took her mind off Clarissa and all her suspicions.

*****

After they left, Megan walked through the house, checking the locks. As she entered the kitchen, she heard a loud commotion on the back porch. Cautiously she took a rolling pin out of the drawer by the stove. Not a great weapon, but it would have to do. It was either that or the old cast-iron skillet from the stove.

She eased open the back door and crept quietly onto the porch. She heard more clattering down at the far end— something rattling around among the empty flower pots.

"Just don't be a skunk; please, please, just don't be a skunk," Megan begged. She could handle a raccoon or possum, but a rolling pin was no protection against the spray from a skunk.

Slowly creeping closer, she realized there was no skunk smell. "Okay, not a skunk." Megan sighed in relief.

Just then, one of the pots toppled over and rolled to Megan's feet. Startled, she jumped back, tripped over a broken lawn rake, and landed hard on the rough, wooden floor of the porch. She sat up and saw a small black kitten with amazing emerald-green eyes crawl out of the pot and looked up at her and mew.

The kitten was only five or six weeks old, not old enough to be alone without its mother.

"You're not a skunk, thank God, but what in heaven's name are you doing out here? You scared the shit out of me." Megan scooped up the shivering little bundle of fur and cuddled it close. The kitten was very hungry and mewed impatiently.

October in New England is wonderful during the day, but the temperature drops at night.

The poor little thing might not survive out here until morning, thought Megan.

"Where did you come from? Where's your mother? Let's see what we can find for you to eat, my furry friend."

Megan took the kitten into the kitchen, locked the door, and made sure the latch caught. She tore up some leftover meat into small pieces and mixed it with a little milk for her newest visitor. The kitten dove into the food; he apparently had not eaten in a while.

Megan found a plastic dishpan and ripped up some newspaper to make a litter tray.

"That will have to do until I decide what to do with you. Please use it." putting the improvised litter pan down next to the food dish. To her surprise, the little kitten crawled into the pan and actually used it. "There is a God! Thank you, thank you."

After cleaning up the kitchen and the glasses used by her and her earlier visitors, Megan was ready for bed. She scooped up the kitten, grabbed the makeshift litter tray, checked the doors again, and climbed the stairs.

Chapter 9

In the morning, Megan woke up to find the kitten fast asleep on the pillow beside her head. "Well, good morning, Fur Ball. Nice to know you don't snore." She showered and dressed, pausing to laugh at the kitten playing with whatever took its fancy. Megan giggled as she watched the kitten try to catch the dust motes that floated in the sunbeams streaming through the window.

Megan brought the kitten down to the kitchen and fed him some more leftovers. She put the kitten and the litter tray in the bathroom, saying, "Not that I don't trust you, but I don't trust you. I'm also not hunting all over the house for you, Fur Ball. So be good and don't destroy anything while I'm gone."

Since it was Sunday, she decided to play tourist for the day, like when she was a kid. She drove the rented Toyota to the Sewell Street parking lot and walked to the tourist trolley stop. She loved the trolley. She could ride all day and hop on and off wherever she liked.

Gran often took Megan to the Salem Witch Trials Memorial. There Megan learned what the fear of the unknown could do. The history of the Salem trials was a source for plays and even an opera. The play *Cry Innocent* had been performed once at Old Town Hall, and her gran had taken her to see it. She also saw the play *The Crucible* in New York. The plays helped make the history of the witch trials come to life for her.

Megan took her time walking along Derby Street. Her grandmother had taken her to every tourist attraction on that street at one time or another. Today she just wandered, remembering what fun she'd had with her beloved Gran.

She took the trolley back to her car and passed the Longstreet Gallery. She made a note to stop there after she visited the lawyer's office tomorrow.

It was nearly dark when she got back to the house. She had stopped to pick up cat food and proper cat litter for Fur Ball. Juggling her purchases, she let herself in and dropped her stuff on the kitchen counter. Fur Ball wrapped himself around her legs, and Megan was afraid she might step on the small cat.

"Wait a minute. I left you in the bathroom. How the hell did you get out?" Megan wondered aloud. She went and checked the bathroom. The door was open, and the well-used litter tray still there. She checked the latch on the door a couple of times. There was no way the cat could have opened it herself.

Megan grabbed Fur Ball and ran across the slippery grass next door to Zack's and Amanda's house.

"I'm so sorry to bother you, but can Zack come over and check the house? I know someone's been in there, and I know I'm being foolish, but I want to be sure they're gone," she stammered when Amanda answered the door.

"Oh, of course, Zack, can you get out here, please?" Amanda called. "Megan says someone has been in the house!" Amanda looked at Megan and said, "Don't worry, he'll check it out."

Zack arrived, pulling on his jacket and clamping his old hat on his head. He grabbed a baseball bat on his way out.

"Let's go find us a boogey man," he called to Megan. He marched across to Megan's house with the bat perched on his shoulder. Megan and Amanda laughed as they watched him, still wearing his cargo shorts and sandals. He made quite a sight.

Megan followed him across the crunching leaves, and together they checked out the old house from cellar to attic, looking in all the closets along the way, sure someone would jump out at them from behind every door they opened.

The cellar held only rusting garden tools, webbed aluminum, folding chairs, and used, dirty terracotta flower pots, But the attic had potential with its old trunks, pictures stacked against the walls, boxes of old books, and a couple of nice, old rocking chairs. It will all need to be cleaned out, thought Megan—another project to add to her growing list.

They didn't find anyone lurking in the house.

She saw Zack to the front door. "I'm so sorry to have bothered you with chasing after nothing. I owe you big time for coming to my rescue tonight."

Zack gave her his phone number. "No problem, you just call or come over anytime."

She promised to call if anything went bump in the night. They both laughed a bit to lighten the mood, and Megan promised to drop by the gallery tomorrow.

"Oh, Lord, Fur Ball, now I know what Gran was going through," she groaned, picking up the little kitten and nuzzling her face in Fur Ball's soft, black fur. "How would you like to split a pizza with me? I'm not cooking tonight."

Later, cozy on the couch with Fur Ball in her lap, Megan fed pepperoni to the kitten and drifted off to sleep watching an old movie on the television.

Chapter 10

The next morning, Megan found the lawyer's office without much trouble. The office of Goldberg and Halloran was in one of Salem's older buildings, and she had to climb up a steep, dark stairway to reach it. The secretary, who introduced herself as Miss Parrish, Julia Parrish, greeted her warmly and expressed her condolences.

"I'm so sorry to hear about your grandmother, Megan. She was always cheerful and easy to talk to, a lovely lady. We had some pleasant chats while she waited to see Mr. Halloran. She was very proud of you and talked about you a lot."

Miss Parrish looked at the clock and back at Megan. "I'll let Mr. Halloran know you're here,

and he'll be right with you." She picked up her phone and announced that Megan was there.

Miss Parrish looked to be somewhere between thirty and forty. Her light brown hair was beginning to have hints of gray. The cut of her hair accented the pale blue eyes behind stylish, thin-framed glasses. Megan wondered why she was still Miss Parrish. She was very attractive in her businesslike way. Even her nails look to be professionally manicured.

I'll bet she makes good money as a lawyer's secretary, thought Megan.

Megan waited only five minutes before Miss Parrish came back and showed her in to see Mr. Halloran.

"Please come in, Megan. Have a seat. I'm sorry about your grandmother. She was a great lady," he said.

"Thank you. So I'm finding out," said Megan.

Mr. Halloran was a handsome man. His hair was graying just at the temples, and he looked very distinguished in his Brooks Brothers suit. When he shook Megan's hand, she noticed the expensive-looking cufflinks on his shirt sleeves and a very expensive Rolex watch. She thought it odd to find such a well-dressed lawyer working in a dingy walk-up office in Salem.

"Well, let's get on with this. Your grandmother left everything in order. We talked things over several times. Basically, she leaves everything to you. There is the house, of course, its contents and a small bank account. Since you're an only child and your mother and father are both deceased, there is no problem with you inheriting it all. The only stipulation your grandmother insisted on was that I give you this little box and letter in person. The box you can open now. You may read the letter at your leisure."

As he spoke, Mr. Halloran pushed a small, green-velvet jewelry box across his desk to

Megan. She took it carefully and gently lifted the lid. Inside was a beautiful gold ring with two hands holding a heart-shaped emerald in the center—an Irish Claddagh ring.

She had never seen this ring before but had seen Claddagh rings and knew they had a rich past, dating back over three hundred years. The design is rooted deep in Irish tradition: The hands symbolize friendship and togetherness, the heart signifies love, and a crown over the heart indicates loyalty.

This ring was special. First of all, it was her gran's, and second, it was absolutely stunning. A gorgeous emerald sparkled in the heart of it.

"Oh, my God, this is beautiful!" Megan gasped. This was not like the other Irish rings she had seen. A lot of people had them. But she experienced a special, strange feeling when she first looked at this one. Like something that had been lost was now found. She didn't remember ever seeing her gran wear it. It was weird that she felt such a strange connection to a bit of jewelry she didn't know existed until now. She closed the box and took a deep breath.

"Sorry, Mr. Halloran, a lot of emotions going on," she said.

"That's understandable, my dear. If you need anything, give me a call. If you need any advice, I'm here. I've been your family attorney for years."

He stood up, walked around the desk, shook Megan's hand, and gave her his card.

"Thank you for everything, Mr. Halloran," she said as she left his office.

Megan thanked Miss Parrish on the way out and said good -bye.

"Good-bye, Megan. I hope you can settle things here in Salem and get back to New York soon."

"Once I clear out the house and put it on the market, I'm off to the Big Apple again."

Broken Branches

Megan walked back down the stairs to the street. She didn't want to go home yet. It was late morning and a lovely Indian summer day—not like the cold, wet weather that would arrive in the coming weeks. She decided to walk down to the wharf, find a bench in the sun and read Gran's letter there.

*****

Just as she picked out a spot to read Gran's letter, she saw the ship Fame cruising into the harbor. The ship brought back another memory of her gran. The two of them enjoyed sailing here every time she visited in the summer.

The schooner was a replica of the original Fame; a fast fishing schooner had been reborn as a privateer when the War of 1812 broke out. She was one of the first American privateers to bring home a prize—a captured British ship—and she brought home twenty more before being wrecked in the Bay of Fundy in 1814. Now the tourists' dollars were her prize.

Megan checked the sailing times at the ticket booth. The next trip out was in an hour—just enough time for a bit of lunch and to read her gran's letter.

Megan found a small café across the marina parking lot. She walked in and settled into a booth. "Hi, I'm Kathy. What can I get you today?" the waitress asked pleasantly.

Megan ordered a lobster roll and iced tea. While she waited, she took the letter out of her purse, took a deep breath, and began to read.

My Dearest Megan,

I hope you like the gift I left for you. That ring was handed down to me by my mother, by her mother, and so on, from mother to daughter through several generations. I hope you will wear it and enjoy the love of all the women who have worn it before you.

There are traditions to wearing the ring. When you're looking for love, the ring is worn on the right hand with the heart pointing away. When you find your love, the ring is moved to the left hand, the heart pointing in. There is magic in love, my dear. Enjoy it.

There is an old trunk up in the attic that contains documents that trace the genealogy of the women that have worn the ring before you. Our line goes back to the Salem of old—all the way to the witch trials.

I have left you the old house and all it contains. It is yours to do with what you want. The house has stories to tell if you but look, and for a special occasion, always wear the green.

I love you, my darling,

Grandma Corey

Okay, Gran, I'll wear the ring proudly because I love it and you, but what the hell does "always wear the green" mean? Megan pondered silently.

As she brought Megan's lunch, the waitress looked at her. "I'm sorry, but do I know you? You look very familiar."

Kathy was about Megan's age. Her hair was twirled up on her head, and she wore the blue uniform and white apron of the café. Across her top breast pocket, "The Dockside Café" was embroidered in white.

"I don't think so, but I might have been in here with my grandmother once upon a time. I'm just here for my grandmother's funeral. I'll be leaving in a couple of weeks."

"Oh, that's too bad. Who was your grandmother? Maybe I know her?"

"Her name was Corey Bishop."

"Yes! I knew her! That's why you look familiar. She showed me a newspaper article about you; it had your picture in it. She was so proud of you. I'm sorry to hear she passed away—I had no idea. She was such a friendly person, always nice to the waitresses, and left decent tips. It's been a while since she came in. I used to tell her the specials. She was having trouble seeing things a bit. We'll all miss her. I'll leave you to your lunch."

Megan had more to digest than just her meal. She finished up her lobster roll, made exactly how it should be with chunks of lobster, a bit of mayo, and served on a toasted New England hot dog roll. She thanked Kathy and left a decent tip, just like Gran would have done.

*****

While Megan ate her lunch, a car idled in the parking lot. Its tinted windows hid the person inside, who nervously tapped the steering wheel. All their careful planning was unraveling. Megan was young and curious, not an almost-blind old lady. They were so close to their goal, and now this problem was in their way.

What do we do with problems? We get rid of them.

Chapter 11

Megan walked out the café door—her mind on her grandmother's letter and trying to get to the ship on time. All of a sudden, someone grabbed her and threw her through the air. A black sedan sped by, barely missing her, spraying gravel as it went.

Megan landed hard on the gravel parking lot with a heavy weight on top of her. It took her a second to realize the weight was a man. "Get off me, you pervert! What the hell do you think you're doing, tackling me like that?" she yelled, trying to push him off.

"I was saving your life if you must know," he replied. "That car almost ran you down. You weren't watching where you were going. I don't think the driver saw you, either. It never slowed and was going much too fast for a parking lot."

"Um, you can get off me now." Megan put her hands on his chest and tried to push him off. She felt a warm body under his shirt and a strange dizzy feeling. Had she met this man before? Her touch on his chest felt so familiar and so right. She looked up into amazing, hazel eyes with flecks of deep green. For a second, her world tipped sideways, and she thought she would pass out.

Struggling not to faint, she tried shoving this sexy stranger off her, and then she started to wonder what it would be like to lose herself in those eyes and in his arms.

He was tall, about six-foot-six, with sandy-colored hair that was being ruffled by the sea breeze. He was dressed in jeans, a casual shirt, and a soft brown leather jacket that showed off his wide shoulders and narrow hips.

"Get off me," she repeated. "In case you haven't noticed, there are no more cars trying to run me over, and we're starting to draw a crowd." This is getting embarrassing, she thought.

He got up, took Megan's hand, and helped her to her somewhat shaky feet. He grinned at Megan. "Sorry, I was rather enjoying it. I don't get to save a beautiful girl every day."

His eyes twinkled, and he tried hard not to laugh. She noticed he had a marvelous way of turning up the corner of his mouth.

What would it be like to kiss that upturned corner? Megan couldn't help wondering.

"Are you going to be okay? You still look a bit shaken up."

Megan noticed he still had hold of her hand.

"Ah, can I have my hand back, please?" she asked— while not wanting him to let go.

"Sorry," he said, releasing her hand. "Wait. Why am I apologizing for saving your life? Look, if you don't need any more saving, I'll be on my way." He reluctantly turned to go.

"Wait, please. I am thankful. I wasn't looking where I was going and had too much on my mind. I was going to take a cruise on the Fame to think things over. I was looking at the ticket booth and not at the car, trying to kill me. I'm the one who should apologize."

"That's just where I was going," he lied. He wanted to spend more time with Megan, and it was a good excuse. She fascinated him. It was more than her looks, although that helped. There was something more that drew him to her, and he wanted to figure it out.

"Come on then. The ship is preparing to cast off and almost ready to go. We can make it if we hurry," taking Megan's hand again Jake, gently pulled her towards the ship.

Together they jogged to the gangplank and ticket booth. Most of the passengers had already boarded. He paid for the tickets over her protest and helped her board the schooner.

She loved anything with sails. They were just so romantic. She could lose herself in the feel of the waves crashing against the hull and the wind in her hair.

Once, when she was young, her parents had taken her to see the tall ships sail into New York Harbor. That was a sight she would never forget. To her, sailing ships were magical. One of her dreams was to take a trip on one of the schooners out of Camden, Maine, sometime.

They found a spot near the bow and settled down as the ship pulled away from the wharf and into the harbor. They sailed quietly for a while as they watched the town slip away.

"Let me introduce myself. I'm Jake Durant. What's your name?"

"I'm Megan, Megan Calloway."

"Hi, Megan, do you often need rescuing from speeding cars?"

"No, I must say that was a first for me. What do you do when you're not rescuing strangers?"

"I write mystery novels and live in Boston. I'm playing tourist for the day, relaxing and doing a bit of research in Salem before I start working again."

Megan listened attentively, loving the sound of his voice and the motion of the ship. She didn't volunteer any information about herself.

"I love it here in Salem this time of year," Jake said. "I love the colors of the trees, the cool, crisp days, and the nip in the air at night. The weeks leading up to Halloween are crazy. I love the ghost tours. I've been on a couple of the evening ones, have you? They're fantastic. Halloween is my favorite holiday, as you can probably guess. Next favorite is Christmas, of course." He paused. "Sorry, I'm talking too much. Now it's your turn."

"I'm sorry. I'm not very good company today. Maybe I should have gone home instead."

"You're from Salem then? You're a local girl taking a cruise on the Fame?"

"I'm from New York. I own an art gallery in the city. My mother grew up here in Salem, but I'm only in Salem for a couple of weeks. My grandmother passed away, and I'm here to settle her affairs."

"I'm sorry to hear about your grandmother. Had she been sick a long time?"

"No, not at all. Your grandmother was having trouble seeing, but otherwise, she was in good health, as far as I know. She fell down the stairs and died. It looks like an accident, but I have reasons to believe that she might have been killed."

"Megan, I don't know what to say. What makes you think she was killed?"

"A friend of hers told me some things that didn't sound right. She said that Gran never used the stairs. She had a bedroom on the ground floor and didn't need to go upstairs for anything. The police are not looking into it, and I've got a feeling that it's more than just an accident.

Megan took a deep breath and continued. "This friend said my gran thought there was a ghost in the house, and now I'm starting to believe she might have been right. It's either a ghost or some very big mice."

Megan felt that Jake was listening to her and found the courage to go on. She needed to talk to someone, and for some strange reason talking to him felt good and right.

"I found a black cat I've named Fur Ball," Megan said with a nervous little giggle. "I don't know why I'm telling you any of this. I'm just rattling on. I must sound like a crazy person."

Megan stood up and started pacing. She turned away from Jake and said, "I don't know you. Except that you saved my life, and, for some reason, I like you. I've said too much, too. I don't usually carry on like this. I better stop now," Megan said, embarrassed all over again, digging in her pockets for a tissue to wipe her eyes.

"Megan, I like you, too," he said, standing up. He put his hands on her shoulders and turned her around to face him. "I don't know why, either." Jake felt a strange connection he'd never felt before. He decided to change the subject.

"Tell me more about your grandmother and the ghosts. You can tell me about Fur Ball, too."

*****

Megan couldn't resist. She sat back down and told Jake everything about her grandmother's unexpected death. The guilt she felt for not keeping in touch with her. She also told him about the doors being opened and the noises in the attic. She told him about her new neighbors, Zack and Amanda, coming to her rescue and checking out the house and finding nothing. How she encountered Fur Ball and how the kitten got out of the bathroom. Jake listened and asked questions encouraging her to talk it all out.

"This morning, I went to the lawyer's office for the reading of the will, and he gave me this ring Gran left for me."

She held out her right hand, and he took it to look at the Claddagh ring on her finger. She felt the world start to slip away again as he touched her hand. She looked into his eyes and felt she had come home. She looked down at their entwined hands, and it seemed like the emerald at the heart of her ring was glowing. She knew it was only a trick of the light—or was it? Lifting her eyes to his again, she knew she wanted him to kiss her and kiss her hard.

Jake lowered his lips to hers. He kissed her gently at first. He didn't want to frighten her. She pulled him into her kiss, and he responded. He kissed her and explored all the sweet softness that was hers to give. Her knees went to jelly, and her insides responded with a desire for much more than this one kiss.

"Oh, my, that was . . . I don't know what it was," Megan stammered, a rosy glow creeping across her cheeks. "I don't know you. We've only just met, and here I am kissing you."

She pushed him away. "Okay, it's official. I'm a hussy kissing strangers I've just met."

"If you need to kiss me again to figure it out, I have no objections," Jake said with a hopeful twinkle in his eye.

"No, I don't think that's a good idea."

Megan turned away to watch the ship return to the wharf. She had to take a deep breath. Maybe she was going crazy. Maybe her Gran had gone crazy, thinking about ghosts and all. This kind of stuff wasn't inherited, was it?

The ship docked back in Salem, and everyone started to disembark. As they left the ship, Megan turned to Jake and said, "I enjoyed talking to you. I needed to unload. The other bit, I'm not sure about. I'm not the type to be kissing strangers. I just don't do things like that."

"We don't have to be strangers. We can be friends. How about we spend the rest of the day together? You like me. I like you. A couple of hours seeing the sights is something that friends do. What do you say?"

Megan thought about his offer for a minute. "Okay, but I say where. I made plans to see Amanda's and Zack's gallery this afternoon. We can start there."

"Deal. What about cars? Who drives?"

"You drive. I left my car up near my lawyer's office. I'll navigate because I know where the gallery is. You can bring me back here after we see it. I want to pick up some clam chowder from the Dockside to take home for supper, anyway. I can walk back and pick up my car afterward."

Jake took her to his sporty silver Mercedes. He opened the passenger-side door for her and helped her in.

Megan turned to him as he sat in the car, "Just friends, right?" She was still not sure she could trust him or where this would all lead.

"Just friends, Megan, that's all." Jake had a feeling that they were going to be more than just friends. Lightning had struck, and he was not going to let her get away.

Chapter 12

Once they got that settled, they drove a couple of blocks over to the Longstreet Gallery. It was not a huge place, but it contained a nice collection of local artwork and sculptures. The Longstreets had a good eye and encouraged local artists.

Each show would run about six weeks, and then they would change things around with all new work. That way, visitors would be encouraged to come back every few weeks to see the new pieces. Zack was great at arranging and hanging the exhibitions, and Amanda was the business person. Together they made a great team.

Jake and Megan were just entering the front door when Zack spotted them.

"Hey, Megan, who have you got there? New in town and picking up guys already?" Zack called.

"This is Jake Durant. He's a writer up from Boston doing some research for a novel he's working on," Megan said, introducing Jake. "This gentleman saved me from getting run down in a parking lot by a speeding car. I thought I'd show him your gallery." Megan was not about to tell Zack about the trip on the schooner and what had happened there.

"You've got a nice place here. Good location, too. How it's doing with the economy the way it is?" Jake asked, hoping to distract Zack from the parking lot incident. It didn't work.

"What do you mean almost got run down in the parking lot? What parking lot? Run down by whom?" Zack asked, thinking about what might have happened.

"It was nothing, just me and the driver not watching where we were going," Megan said.

"Well, I hope you're not going to make a habit of it. My nerves couldn't take it," said Zack.

Jake, still trying to divert Zack, asked him for a tour of the gallery. "How about showing us around?"

"Sure thing! Well, we're not doing too badly," Zack said. "It could be better, but we manage to pay the bills. Some of the smaller galleries have gone under, but so far, we're okay. Come back here—I've got something to show Megan." Zack led them into the main part of the gallery.

There, centered on the wall, was a portrait of a young lady, circa 1850. She wore a beautiful emerald-green dress, a gold-and-emerald necklace, and matching earrings. On her left hand, she wore a Claddagh ring with an emerald heart.

"What do you think? It was here when we bought the place." Zack turned around and did a double-take as he looked from the portrait to Megan. "That's you! How can that be?"

"I knew you looked familiar when we met!" exclaimed Amanda, who had come out of her office to join them. "I told Zack there was a resemblance, but this is unreal."

Megan had gone deathly pale and started to sway. Jake caught her and guided her to a bench nearby. "Do you need to see a doctor? That's the second time you've almost passed out on me today."

"What's this about passing out twice? Megan, are you alright?" There was concern, loud and clear in Amanda's voice. Amanda liked Megan and considered her a friend.

"I'm not sure. I think I'm fine, but I'm getting scared. Something is going on here. I didn't want to say anything because you'll all think I'm nuts."

"We need to get to the bottom of this. What are you holding out on us?" Jake said gently, looking her straight in the eyes. Megan leaned into him and tried to explain what she had been experiencing.

"It started when I was in the lawyer's office. He handed me a jewelry box, and as I opened it, I saw the open box being handed to me by a man, but it wasn't my lawyer. I saw only a man's hands holding it. As I opened the box and took the ring out of it, I got dizzy.

"A little while later, I met Jake. When he saved me from that car, and we were on the ground, I felt I had met him before, and I already knew how he felt, I mean knew the feel of his body. Today has been so strange for me; I don't know what's happening. And look—my ring is identical to the one in the portrait. What's going on here?"

Megan held out her hand, and all of them agreed it was the same ring.

"Jake and I took a trip on the Fame before coming here. He took my hand to look at the ring. I got dizzy again, and this time I saw Jake standing at the bottom of the stairs in

Gran's house. I was at the top of the stairs looking down at him."

"Are you sure you're not weak from hunger? Did you eat today?" Zack asked.

Amanda hit him on the top of his bald head and said, "Would you shut up and listen? This is fascinating. Wait— saved you from what car?"

"I'll tell you later," Zack whispered.

Megan left out the kissing bit. It was something she was not ready to tell Zack and Amanda about, at least not until she had time to figure it out herself.

"Yes, I had breakfast and lunch, and I don't get seasick. We were just talking and having a good time."

She glanced at Jake with a small smile on her lips. There were some secrets to keep.

Amanda caught the exchange and decided there was more to that trip than Megan was letting on. Amanda was sharp and would get it out of Megan sooner or later. She poked Zack in the ribs, and he gave her a "What's that for?" look. Zack, you're so dense, Amanda thought. She would fill him in later.

"When we got here, to the gallery, I was fine, but then I saw that portrait and got dizzy. I saw myself sitting before a mirror. I was wearing that dress and necklace and was putting on the earrings. There was a small, colorful bouquet on the dressing table, and the ring was sitting in the open box. I felt I was dressing for a special occasion. I'm sorry," Megan said, wiping tears from her eyes.

"I don't know what's going on or why I'm crying. I'm just so glad I have you guys to talk to. Even that's nuts because I just met Zack and Amanda a couple of days ago, and I don't know you at all, Jake, but I feel like we've been friends or something for a very long time."

Megan was really afraid that she was losing her mind. She had never been the type to have dizzy spells and visions or go around kissing strangers. She didn't even know if the visions were of the past or the future. The future didn't make sense because the dress and earrings existed long ago. It had to be about the past, but why? What did it mean?

"Listen to me," Jake said. "I'm not leaving Salem with you like this. If you let me, I'll stay in the house with you until we can figure it out. I agree something is going on, and it's more than just ghosts or uninvited guests invading your grandmother's house."

Amanda had been staring at Jake, trying to place him. She had seen him before, but where? Suddenly it came to her. She jumped up and ran to her office. "I knew it, I knew it! I know who he is," she exclaimed as she ran.

"What the hell was that all about?" Zack called after her. "You know who 'who' is, Amanda? What are you talking about?"

Amanda came back, breathing hard, clutching a book in her hands. "Look! Look, it's him! Jackson Durant, the mystery writer. He's writing about Salem. The name sounded familiar, but Jake, instead of Jackson. It took a while before it clicked."

She turned and faced Jake. "I've read all your novels and seen all the made-for-TV movies they made out of your books. You're a famous author, and you're in my gallery!" Amanda held up the book and pointed to Jake's photo on the back. There could be no mistake.

"Okay, 'fess up," Zack said. "Just how famous are you—local famous or worldwide famous? Are you rich?"

"Zack, quit," Amanda scolded. "My turn! Jake, will you sign my book, please? I never met a famous author before."

"One question at a time, please!" Jake said, laughing at their excitement. "I don't consider myself famous. It's just a job to me. I've made the bestseller list a couple of times. Writing gives me enough to live comfortably. It's work, but also fun. Researching a story, I sometimes get to travel. I meet some very interesting people along the way."

He glanced at Megan and smiled. "And, yes, Amanda, I'll sign your book."

"Okay, you're famous, and I'm nuts," Megan said. "I'm going to let you stay with me for a couple of days—only because I'm really scared. Someone is roaming around the house; there are ghosts, or I'm ready for the funny farm. Take your pick."

Amanda left them and went to talk to a visitor who had just come in.

Megan and Jake stayed and talked with Zack for a bit longer and then headed back to the Dockside Café. Megan picked up some clam chowder, and Kathy tucked in some freshly made yeast rolls for them. Jake stopped at a nearby drug store to buy a toothbrush, toothpaste, some shaving cream, and disposable razors, which he hadn't thought he would need when he left Boston for the day. They headed to the lawyer's office to pick up Megan's car, and then Jake followed Megan to her grandmother's home.

Chapter 13

Megan let them in the front door and walked back to the kitchen. Fur Ball greeted them, winding himself around their legs and calling for his supper.

"So this is Fur Ball," Jake said. He picked up the small black cat and gazed at its face. "What a cute little thing. I've never seen a cat with green eyes before. They're the color of emeralds."

"They are unusual, aren't they?" Megan said. "And he sure looks hungry! I am, too. I'll heat the chowder, and we can eat in the sitting room if you don't mind. Can you get a couple of bowls down from that cupboard to the right of the sink? Then you have to tell me all about your life as a famous mystery writer."

While Megan prepared dinner, Jake lit a rolled-up newspaper to test the fireplace draft. It seemed to draw well, so he deemed it safe enough, and he lit a small fire. They ate and then spent the rest of the evening talking in front of the dancing flames. Fur Ball turned traitor and curled up, purring, in Jake's lap.

After a bit, they cleaned up the dishes and got a room ready for Jake. Megan chose one down the hall from hers. She wanted him close, but not too close. After that kiss on the schooner, she just didn't trust herself. What if she started sleep-walking and ended up in his room? What if she thought she was dreaming but wasn't? A hundred "what ifs" went through her mind as she went to her room—alone.

*****

The next morning, after breakfast, the doorbell chimed. Megan answered it cautiously.

"Hello. You must be Megan, Mrs. Bishop's granddaughter. I'm Mr. Prendergast. I was talking to your grandmother about buying the house. May I come in and talk to you about it?"

Megan asked him in, although she didn't want to. After her conversation with Clarissa, she was on her guard.

Prendergast was a comical figure, reminding Megan of Humpty Dumpty, of all things. He was only five-foot-eight and weighed at least three hundred pounds. His comb-over simply highlighted his bald head, and the dark-rimmed glasses slipping down his nose had not been in fashion for years. His suit jacket could not button over his rotund belly, and the crooked bow tie he wore completed the effect. Megan had a hard time not laughing at her visitor's strange appearance.

"Have a seat, and I'll be right back. Would you like a cup of coffee or anything?" Megan asked. Gran would want her to mind her manners.

"Coffee would be fine, thanks—milk and three sugars, please."

Megan rushed to the kitchen to get Jake. She was trying so hard not to laugh that she was having a hard time talking.

"What's up with you?" he asked. He set his coffee mug on the table, and Fur Ball jumped into his lap and nudged his hand to be petted.

"You have got to come out here. Mr. Prendergast is here about buying Gran's house. I still have no idea what I'm going to do." As she talked, she poured coffee into a mug and added the milk and three sugars. "I want to sell, I think, but I've also thought about keeping it. Then I ask myself why I'd want to. It's way too big for just me. The maintenance alone would break me.

Besides, I own an art gallery in New York! Oh, this is ridiculous. Please come with me to talk to this guy."

"No problem. Let's go see what the toad is offering."

Together they walked back to Mr. Prendergast. "Don't burst out laughing when you meet him. He's a bit odd-looking," whispered Megan.

"Here's your coffee, Mr. Prendergast. This is my friend Jake Durant. I've asked him to join us. I hope you don't mind."

"That's fine, Megan. I don't mind at all. As I said, I talked to your grandmother several times about buying this old ark of a house. It is in great need of some very extensive and expensive repair work. She could never make up her mind. I'm prepared to make you the same offer."

"Mr. Prendergast, may I ask why you want this old ark of a house'?" Megan asked—using his own words.

"Certainly. I believe in being honest with the people I buy from," he said. "People don't want these big houses with all the upkeep. Families are smaller and don't need six bedrooms and a big plot of land to take care of. I buy these big places and turn them into condos. Some I tear down and start from the ground up. Some I'm able to salvage by remodeling them into condos. The market for smaller residences is especially good this close to Boston. It's an easy commute for the business professional looking to live outside the busy city."

"I appreciate your honesty, Mr. Prendergast," said Megan, still not sure she trusted him. "So what are you offering? I haven't decided whether or not to sell, but I want to get other offers, too. I'm not going to take the first offer that comes along. I still have a lot of work to do, going through and clearing out Gran's belongings. I've only just started calling antique dealers and the Goodwill."

"Mr. Prendergast, why don't you put your offer in writing so Megan can think it over for a few days? Meanwhile, she can get a couple more offers to compare. Selling the house is a big decision to make, and Megan doesn't want to rush it," Jake said, taking the pressure off Megan.

"I understand," he said, turning to Megan. "But your grandmother could not make up her mind, either, and I've been waiting very patiently.

There are other properties I could buy, but I liked your grandmother and hoped to make her see reason. Unfortunately, she passed before we could come to an agreement. I'll send you my offer tomorrow and will only wait until the end of October for an answer. If you don't accept my offer by then, I'll move on to someone else."

As Mr. Prendergast struggled to get up from his seat, he reminded Megan of a pregnant woman. He picked up his briefcase and presented his card to Megan. "I hope to hear from you soon."

Megan and Jake showed him to the door and watched him waddle to his late-model BMW.

As they closed the door behind him, Jake and Megan broke out laughing. It took several minutes for them to be able to stop. Every time they looked at one another, they would start to laugh all over again. It didn't help when Jake imitated Mr. Prendergast waddling to his car. Megan was laughing so hard tears were running down her face. "Jake, stop! You're killing me! My sides can't take anymore."

"Okay, I'll be good." Jake put his arm around Megan's shoulders as they walked back to the kitchen.

*****

Jake broke the silence first. "Well, did that help any? He sounded like he was telling the truth. He was very upfront about why he wanted the house and what he might do with it."

Jake didn't want to pressure Megan to sell or keep the house. It had to be her decision. He wanted to be helpful and supportive. But he knew what he wanted her to do. He hoped she would keep the house and stay in Salem. He didn't want her to go back to New York. He liked her. He liked her a lot. Hell, he might even be falling in love with her. Damn, damn and double damn, who was he fooling? He fell in love right there in the parking lot of the wharf. The moment he touched her, he was a goner.

"Mr. Prendergast gives me the creeps, plain and simple," said Megan. "I don't trust him. What if he's the one that tried to drive Gran crazy?"

"Can you see him sneaking around the house? Think about it," Jake chuckled.

"No, but he could hire someone to do it. Oh, never mind, I can't think about that right now," Megan said as she picked up her to-do list. "I have an antique dealer coming in an hour to look over some of Gran's things. You know, I hate having to do all this. I just want my Gran back. I want her here to help me through this. I'm mad at her for dying on me." Megan collapsed on a kitchen chair and started to cry.

Jake sat down in a chair next to her, putting his arm around her and pulling her close. Tenderly he raised her head and looked into her eyes.

"You're right. Selling the house is a tough decision, but you're tough, too. I'll be here to help as much as you'll let me. Megan, I'm in love with you. It's happened so fast, and for whatever mysterious reason, we found each other, but it feels so right."

He lowered his lips to hers and kissed her gently. He deepened his kisses and felt her respond. Kissing her was not going to be enough, but for now, it had to be. He drew back and looked at her. Megan still had her eyes closed. Softly he kissed her eyelids. When she opened her eyes, he saw that she loved him, too. "Megan, we don't have time to finish what I'd like to do now. Tonight we can take all the time we need."

*****

The morning went by fast. The antique dealer came and gave Megan an idea of which pieces might fetch a good price should she decide to sell them. Goodwill also would be getting Gran's clothes and gently used furniture.

Her gran's china cabinet was full of valuable things: The Waterford crystal, china, and sterling silver brought the total up, but she would never sell the cabinet's contents. She just wanted to know the worth of what was in it for insurance purposes.

In the kitchen pantry, she found several more Waterford vases, which made her wonder what else she might find hidden away.

They broke for lunch and decided to go to the café where they had met. Kathy greeted them warmly and served them again.

"Hey, glad to see you two together. After that trouble in the parking lot, I didn't think I'd see either one of you again. How about some iced tea while you look at the menu?"

Jake ordered a cheeseburger, and Megan wanted fried clams. While she was here, she would indulge in all the regional things she couldn't get easily in New York. No telling when she would get back up this way again.

They talked a bit about what else needed to be done to the house. So far, they had only touched the downstairs. Big surprises could be in store when they tackled the basement—and especially the attic. Megan gave Jake her gran's letter to read.

"I see what you mean. Gran gets very cryptic at the end. I can't figure out what 'always wear the green' means, either."

Kathy appeared with their tea and took their order. Tapping her pen on her order pad, she asked, "You remember I said you looked familiar when you were here before? Well, I remembered. There's a painting in the Longstreet Gallery that looks exactly like you. I took my aunt there. She likes art galleries and that kind of stuff. It took me a bit to put it together. You have to go see it."

"We have seen it," Megan said. "Who knows? Maybe it's a distant relative. The Longstreets are going to do some digging and see what they can come up with."

"You need to go see Clarissa at the Salem Museum. I'll bet she could look up some old records. It'd be kind of neat if it were a relative. Are you going to put the old place up for sale? Sorry, I get carried away. I've always been the nosy type. It's none of my business. You just get to know people, and they talk a bit, and I listen. I'll get your order."

"No problem," Megan said, leaving Kathy to put in their lunch orders.

"It's a good idea, though," said Jake. "Going to meet this Clarissa person and seeing what she can uncover. If there's nothing on that list of yours for this afternoon, we could go after lunch."

"We might as well. I'm tired of digging in closets and cupboards for today. I also need to think about Mr. Prendergast's offer.

"I'll call a couple more agents to see what I could get for the house should I decide to sell it. It is too big for just one person."

"I've had some thoughts about that as well," said Jake, as Kathy brought their lunch.

"Sure hope you folks don't mind me being chatty and sticking my nose in. I just feel like I know you because of your gran and all," Kathy said again.

"Don't worry about it, Kathy. I don't have many friends here, and I like talking to you, too," Megan said, dipping a golden fried clam into some tartar sauce. Jake was already attacking his cheeseburger. "Maybe later you can fill me in on a couple of people around here."

"Sure. I know just about everybody. If they're local, they usually end up in here at some point."

Megan and Jake carried on eating and talking about what was still on Megan's list. Tomorrow she planned to call the Goodwill to pick up her gran's clothes, some old books, and other bits and pieces. Megan also had to call The Junk Hunks to cart away many things in the basement and other stuff. She felt she finally was getting a grip on cleaning out the house.

Jake paid Kathy for lunch, and then he and Megan made their way to the Salem Museum on Derby Square to meet with Clarissa. It was on the site of Salem's Old Town Hall and was a wonderful place for history buffs. It contained lots of information on the witch trials, names and dates, how the trials started, and other details about early Salem. It was amazing that people were still fascinated with the witch trials after over three hundred years. Tourists came all year round, but there was something special about Salem at Halloween.

Chapter 14

Megan and Jake walked into the Salem Museum, and Megan told the receptionist that they were there to see Clarissa. The receptionist showed them to a back office, where Clarissa was seated behind an old desk, her polished red nails clicking away on her computer.

Even her glasses matched one of the bright colors from the print in her long skirt. Her hair, still a bright red, contained an elaborate peacock-green bow and feather.

Clarissa looked up and exclaimed, "Megan, my dear! How nice to see you. I'm so glad you decided to come and talk to me! And just who is this handsome gentleman with you?"

"Clarissa, this is my friend, Jake. He's helping me clear out the house." Megan didn't want to go into how she had met Jake or say that he was staying at the house with her. She didn't know Clarissa well enough to go into such personal information, and, in the long run, it was no one's business but her own.

"Hello, Clarissa, nice to meet you," Jake said as he shook Clarissa's hand. "Megan has told me a little about your conversation at the wake and the funeral. We've already had a visit from Mr. Prendergast about the house."

"That snake!" said Clarissa. "I don't trust him as far as I could throw him—which, knowing his size—wouldn't be that far at all. I hope you didn't agree to sell to him?" she asked, turning to Megan, very worried that she had been persuaded to sell to Prendergast.

"No, I didn't sell to him. In fact, I'm calling other real estate agents to get an idea of what I could get for the house should I decide to sell."

"Decide to sell? Does that mean that you might keep the old house?" asked Clarissa. "I'd love it to stay in the family—but do you want such a big house all to yourself? The upkeep alone would drive you to the poor house. You're only an artist, and I know Corey could not have left you much money. How could you possibly even think of keeping the place?" Clarissa asked.

Jake jumped to Megan's defense. "The decision is really up to Megan, and she hasn't made up her mind yet," he said, even though he, too, still hoped she would decide to keep the old house.

"Oh, I don't mean to interfere. I just care about Megan. I was her gran's friend for many years. I guess I'm just trying to look after her like Corey would want me to."

"I appreciate that, Clarissa," Megan nodded. "Now, you said you wanted to talk to me about Gran and the spooky happenings in the house?"

"Please have a seat, and I'll start at the beginning." Clarissa took a deep breath and began. "Corey was losing her sight and ability to get around in that big old house. I encouraged her to hire some help, but she was a stubborn New Englander and had to do it on her terms. She made me mad sometimes. I was afraid for her, living there all alone. I did arrange some cleaning help for her once, and she fired them that same week.

"She told me that she would hear noises—like someone moving things around in the basement or the attic. She found that objects were left in unusual places or doors were open that she thought she had locked.

"Then a few months ago, this creep, Prendergast, shows up and wants to buy her house. I recommended selling it but suggested she get an independent appraisal of the property before she did anything. I offered to help her find someone to do it, but she said she'd do it herself.

"The noises in the house disturbed her a lot. She didn't know if an intruder was roaming around the house, if she heard things that weren't there, or if she was going crazy. I stayed with her a couple times and never heard a thing out of the ordinary. That only made Corey feel worse and convinced her that she was losing it.

"Meanwhile, Prendergast kept coming around pressuring her to sell. The worry and stress were taking their toll. That's why she wanted to speak with you, Megan, about what she should do with the house. I think she was leaning toward selling it, but not to Prendergast. She wanted it to stay a family home. The thought of it being turned into condos made her sick.

"I know she called you the morning she died. She called me right before she called you and said she was trying to get you to come up for a visit. I was so pleased that she was going to talk to you.

"Corey had not been upstairs in that house in years. She used the downstairs back room, the one-off the kitchen, as her bedroom, so she had no reason to go up there. Why she would have been on the stairs to fall that morning, I can't imagine. I firmly believe she was pushed down those stairs. I just wish she had called you sooner. I miss her terribly." Clarissa took off her glasses to wipe her tearful eyes.

Jake handed Clarissa a tissue from a box on the desk. "From what you are telling us and what Megan has already been experiencing, I think something is going on in the house," he commented.

"That morning, while I was talking to her, she got distracted by a noise she heard. She said she would talk to me later and hung up. It was very strange," Megan added.

"There's something else," Clarissa said. "While I was poking around in Corey's family history, I found some interesting things. The first was that Corey's family was related to Martha Corey, one of the last people prosecuted in the Salem witch trials. Martha came to Salem as Giles Corey's third wife. The Corey name was passed down through the family, in the latter years as a first or middle name, which is how your grandmother got the name."

Clarissa took a sip from her bottle of water and continued. "I also found some records about some cousins coming over from Ireland about 1848, which would have been during the Irish Potato Famine. They would have been very poor. Most stayed around Boston or New York, but a few moved farther afield."

"I had wondered about her name," said Megan. "I'd never heard of a female with that first name before." Megan held Jake's hand for comfort, which did not go unnoticed by Clarissa.

"Martha Corey's descendants prospered in the area for the next hundred years or so. They made out quite well in the shipping trade and were much respected in the area. In about the 1850s, one of the daughters married a wealthy merchant here in Salem.

"Those two built the house your grandmother lived in. Like the Corey name, the house has been passed down through the family. What's very interesting is that there was talk about a fortune of some sort that was lost or hidden. I can't find a record of anything of great value that was sold. The records show a couple of land transactions, ships that were bought or sold, that sort of thing. I just haven't found out what this phantom fortune was supposed to have been.

"I got to thinking that maybe what's going on in the house has to do with the lost fortune. Someone is poking around, trying to find it or some information about it."

"That makes so much sense!" Megan exclaimed, looking at Jake. "Someone's searching the house. That's why I keep finding the doors unlocked and Fur Ball out of the bathroom."

"I think you're right," said Jake. "Whoever it is has gotten a key somehow and goes through the house when they don't think anyone is there.

They weren't that careful when your gran was alive because she wouldn't have been much of a threat if she had caught them.

Then Jake said what they all were thinking. " I'll bet she did catch someone, and they killed her for it."

"Could she have given a key to Prendergast?" Megan asked.

"I don't think she would have, but you never know," Clarissa said.

Megan got up to pace around the office. "We can't see Prendergast stealthily searching the house. Could he have hired someone to do it?"

"Who besides you and Megan's grandmother knew about this mysterious fortune?" asked Jake. "Did Mrs. Bishop maybe tell someone else, even in passing? That's who we're looking for."

Standing behind Megan's chair, he placed his hands on her shoulders and said, "We can figure this out together."

Megan and Jake said good-bye to Clarissa and promised to keep in touch. On their way back to the house, they stopped to pick up onions, zucchini, and eggplant for a ratatouille to add to the pasta and sauce Amanda had left. They picked up more cat food for Fur Ball as well.

*****

Jake carried everything into the kitchen and started unloading the groceries. Megan put food down for Fur Ball to distract him from winding around their ankles. As she did so, Megan noticed the voicemail light was blinking on the phone. Turning it on, she heard:

"Damn, Megan, this is Jennifer. Don't you ever answer your cell phone? One of the exhibitors for the new display has pulled out, and we need to fill the space. Can you get back to me as soon as possible with some names to try calling? I hope you can come back soon. We need you here. Call me."

Megan dug her cell out of her purse and realized it needed to be charged. "Jake, I've got to call Jennifer at the gallery. There's a file in my office she needs." Megan sighed. "I have to get this mess here sorted out so I can get back to my life in New York."

Jake set the eggplant down on the counter and turned to Megan. "What about us?" he asked softly. He took Megan by the hand and looked her in the eyes. "I thought we were going someplace? This morning we were talking. Or at least I thought we might be. Oh, I don't know what I was thinking. I said I loved you, and you said you loved me, too. I want to be part of your life. Do you want me as part of that life of yours?"

"Right now, I don't know what I want," Megan said. "It's all too much too fast. Gran dying, decisions about selling the house or not, Clarissa's wild suspicions and

Prendergast's pressure, meeting you, and falling for you. When I was in New York at the gallery, everything was so simple. I knew exactly what I was doing. I had my friends, and my future was all mapped out. I don't want to lose all that, but I don't want to lose you, either. I'm so confused. I need time to figure it all out."

"Megan, we can figure it out together," Jake said. "If you want your gallery and me in New York, then that's where we'll be. I can work anywhere. I don't want to lose you because of a location."

Megan leaned in and rested her head on Jake's chest. "I'm out of my depth here," Megan said. "I never had to make the hard choices before. Everything was planned for me—college and the gallery. Now, Gran might have been murdered. An intruder is sneaking around the house.

A Humpty Dumpty look-a-like wants to turn this grand old house into condos. Who do I trust? Who do I believe? Hell, I need a drink."

"Sounds like a good idea, but after supper, okay? We can light a fire and have that drink, maybe more than one," Jake said as he drew Megan close and kissed the top of her head.

Megan went to call Jennifer, and Jake continued getting their supper ready.

Jake turned out to be a very good cook. He made a simple pasta dish seem like a feast, and the aroma of onions and Italian sausage being sautéed in olive oil filled the air.

"That smells wonderful!" Megan said when she returned to the kitchen. "I'm impressed."

"I learned to cook from my mom. I enjoy doing it and living alone; I can experiment all I want. I even thought of going to culinary school to be a chef, but it turned out I was a pretty good mystery writer, so I write for a living and cook for fun."

Megan thought about what Jake had just said. "Are you sticking around so you can use all this trouble for a new mystery novel? Is that what this is all about? Bang the bimbo and get a story out of it?"

Megan tossed a glass into the sink, and it shattered. She grabbed the counter, closed her eyes, and started to sob.

Chapter 15

"Oh, Jake, I'm so sorry. I'm just tired and cranky. It's all getting to me. I don't know who to trust."

Jake took Megan's hands off the counter and turned her around and into his arms. He kissed the salty tears on her cheeks."You can trust me, Megan," Jake said. "I'm not going anywhere. I fell in love with you there on the ground of the parking lot. It was like getting hit with lightning.

"The mystery is just a bonus. I would love you no matter what. I want to spend the rest of my life with you. There, I said it. I love you. Marry me, now, this week. Better still, let's have a Halloween wedding. Invite the few friends we have here. Let's have the wedding right here, in this house. Please, Megan, say yes."

Before Megan could catch her breath and even think about what Jake had just said, the doorbell rang, startling them both.

"Damn it, and I'm not letting this go. I meant every word," Jake said as he released her and went to see who had interrupted them. "I'm going to disconnect that damn doorbell."

Zack and Amanda stood on the doorstep with a surprise present. "We talked it over and want you to have it," said Zack, as he pushed his way in, followed closely by Amanda.

"Yes, we figured it's yours and should be in the house where it belongs," said Amanda.

"What are you two talking about?" Jake asked.

"Why, the portrait of the Lady in Green, of course," Zack said—unwrapping the large painting. "It will be perfect over the big fireplace. It probably hung there years ago when it was first painted. Some family members must have loaned it to the gallery, and it was forgotten about all these years. After seeing the resemblance between you and the lady in the painting, we know it belongs here, Megan." Zack headed into the study to hang the portrait over the fireplace.

"After seeing you faint after seeing it, we think there's magic at work here. It's almost Halloween, and you're in Salem. It all fits!" Amanda said, giddy with excitement.

"Whoa there, who said I want the Lady in Green in my house? You can keep it in the gallery. I don't need to be fainting every time I walk into this room," Megan said, blocking Zack's path to the fireplace.

"Megan, wait," Jake said. "There's writing on the back of the painting."

Chapter 16

Jake took the portrait from Zack and turned it around so they all could look at the back. "It's faint, but it's there."

Megan turned on a table lamp to get a better look. "You're right. Zack, Amanda, has this writing always been here?"

"I don't remember. We found it in a closet and hung it on the wall, where it's been ever since," Zack said.

"This is killing me. What's it say, for pity's sake already?" asked Amanda, trying to get a closer look at the writing.

"Okay, I'll read it," said Megan. "Give me more light so I can see."

Jake held the lamp closer. The writing was very old and faded, making the script hard to read.

"I think it says, *'The key to fortune can be found where friendship and togetherness hold your heart—loyalty guards over all. The lock is in the branches of the tree where ancestors can be found. A symbol of a faraway past guards the green.'*"

"Oh, foo, I hate riddles!" exclaimed Amanda.

"Listen, stay for supper," said Jake. "We'll hang the portrait; I'll throw a salad together to go with the pasta and ratatouille, and we'll try to figure this out. Is that okay with you, Megan?"

Megan nodded that it was.

While they all pitched in with dinner preparations, Megan and Jake brought Amanda and Zack up to speed on what they had found out from Clarissa at the history museum.

Jake seemed to have forgotten the conversation he had started with Megan—at least for now. Megan was glad Zack and Amanda had shown up, so she had a reason to put off answering Jake's question. But she was distracted all evening thinking about what he had asked.

Did she love Jake? Yes, she did. Did she want to spend the rest of her life with him? Yes, she did. Then why was the question about marrying him so hard to answer? Her head told her it was because she met him only three days ago, even though she felt as if she had spent a lifetime with him already.

"Oh, my head hurts with trying to keep all this straight," Amanda groaned.

The two couples had been talking all evening, and it was getting late. The painting of the Lady in Green looked perfect over the fireplace. Megan was glad she could look at it now without fainting.

"We'd better be going," Zack said. "We do have a gallery to run. By the way, we have an opening next Friday evening. We hope you both can come. A great new painter from Derry, Richard Downey—maybe you've heard of him?—agreed to exhibit with us. He's shipping his artwork, and it should be here tomorrow. And it's only a little over a week till Halloween. How about we get together and trick all the little monsters that come out for candy that night?

Amanda and I love Halloween. It's the best holiday of the year."

"Zack goes a bit over the top for Halloween. He's got all kinds of props and stuff for the yard, and I decorate the house inside. You guys up for a party at our house?" Amanda asked hopefully. She liked Megan and Jake and wished they could always be neighbors.

Megan started to answer, but Jake beat her to it. "We'd love to, but we might have other plans. We'll let you know."

*****

After their guests had left, Megan turned to Jake. "Other plans? What other plans?"

"Earlier, I asked you a question, and I meant it," Jake said. Again he took Megan by the shoulders and looked straight into her eyes.

Megan went all weak at the knees and realized that she loved him, too, and knew in her heart that she wanted to spend the rest of her life with him. "I know it's insane and crazy and stupid, but yes. I'll marry you."

At that moment, Megan knew this was meant to be. "You told Zack and Amanda that you had other plans for Halloween night. What exactly did you mean?"

Jake had a curious twinkle in his eyes.

"You're up to something," Megan said. "A party at their house would be fun, and we could make a big announcement with all our friends there."

"I thought we might have the party here and not only announce our plans for the future but actually get married on Halloween," Jake said.

"This Halloween, Are you mad?" Megan argued. "Do you know what it takes to pull off a wedding? Besides, I just buried my grandmother. It's not proper. It's too soon."

"We can do it. Just keep it small. Call a caterer for the food and drinks. Get the cleaning team in again. Just think about it. I love you so much," Jake countered.

"Jake, a wedding, no matter how small, will still cost money. I'm not working right now, and I don't have an endless supply of cash. I still might have to go back to New York. The gallery will only run itself for so long. My staff is great, but I'm the owner, and I need to be there making the decisions. I'd like to do it right."

"I'm a famous writer, remember? I'll pay for anything you want, and after the house is all settled, we can go back to New York if you want to. You can even pay me back if you insist."

"And just how do you want me to pay you back, Mr. Durant?" Megan raised her eyebrows and shot him a knowing glance.

"Why don't you come on upstairs with me now?" Jake asked. "We can start working on the payments right away."

Giggling, Megan took off up the stairs. She called back, "I think I'm going to like working on making those payments!"

Jake charged up after her, taking the steps two at a time. He was going to enjoy the payments as well. "Careful. I might charge interest, too."

Chapter 17

It took Jake a minute for Megan's words to register.

"Shush, let me listen." He rubbed the sleep from his eyes.

"There—there it is again. Like someone moving something heavy across a floor."

They both sat up in bed and listened. There was a definite scuffling, scraping sound of things being moved.

"Stay here," Jake ordered. He went over to his briefcase and pulled out a gun.

Megan cringed. "What the hell are you doing with that thing?"

"Your weapon of choice might be a rolling pin or fry pan, but not mine," he said with a grin. Jake had carried the Glock for quite a few years now and practiced at a firing range as often as he could. He had had some scary run-ins with crazy fans and preferred carrying heat to hiring bodyguards.

Jake moved quietly out of the room and down the hallway to the attic door. He opened the door slowly. Luckily it didn't creak. He made his way up the stairs to where he could just peek through the banister, his head even with the attic floor.

He saw a shadowy figure looking carefully over, under, and behind all the piles of junk that had been accumulated in the attic over decades. The figure came to an old trunk and lifted the lid, and began to shuffle through some papers stored there.

Fur Ball, who had followed Jake up the stairs, rubbed up against Jake's ankles and picked this moment to start meowing. The mysterious visitor turned at the sound and saw Jake. A barrage of bullets flew past Jake's head, narrowly missing him. Jake managed to return a couple of shots at the fleeing intruder and took off after him.

Megan screamed when she heard gunshots ring out. She flew out of bed and down the hall. She slowed down when she reached the attic door. The smell of cordite was strong in the musty attic air.

"Jake! Jake, answer me! What happened? Where are you?" She crouched as she climbed the stairs, holding her breath, waiting for more shots. "Jake, you better answer me, or the wedding is off," she whispered.

She nearly jumped out of her skin when a hand touched her shoulder from behind.

"It's okay. He's gone," Jake said, grabbing and encircling her with his arms. Megan began to cry with relief.

"Wait," she said, pushing him away. "Where the hell did you come from? How did you come up the stairs behind me? Weren't you in the attic getting shot at? Why were you getting shot at? Who were you shooting at?" A million questions flew through her mind.

"Come with me, and I'll play a little show and tell." Jake led her up the rest of the stairs to the attic and across to where a large, tall dresser stood against the wall. Jake walked behind the dresser and disappeared.

"Jake, come on, you're scaring me!" Megan was shaking from the fear-driven adrenalin that was coursing through her. Jake reappeared, and she took a breath.

"Come around here. I've found out how our mystery trespasser has been getting in and out of the house."

Megan followed him behind the old dresser. There, hidden away, was a door with stairs leading down. They groped their way down the dark stairs, guided only by the light from the open door at the bottom. They came out in her grandmother's bedroom. The door was camouflaged by the floral pattern in the wallpaper and hidden by the furniture around it.

"This is how our intruder has been able to get around the house without being seen. I have no way of knowing if your gran knew about this passage to the attic or not, but I'm sure this is how he was able to scare and frighten her into thinking she might be going a bit senile or hearing ghosts."

We need to call the cops," Megan said, collapsing on her gran's bed.

"Tomorrow will be time enough. Whoever it was is gone, so there is nothing the police can do tonight. We'll call them first thing in the morning, and I want to talk with Clarissa again, too."

"Why do you want to talk with Clarissa? Do you think it was her rummaging around the attic and firing shots at you?" Megan asked.

"No, but she might be able to tell us who might know about the back stairs to the attic." Jake sat down beside

Megan and pulled her to him. "Let's go back to bed and try and get some sleep."

Fur Ball jumped up on Gran's bed, purring and rubbing against them with his tail in the air.

"I don't know why you're so happy. You almost got me shot tonight, you little feline troublemaker."

Megan scooped up Fur Ball and buried her face in the soft fur, and together they walked back upstairs for what was left of the night.

Chapter 18

Jake called the police, who arrived right after Megan and Jake had their first cup of coffee. A forensic team started to go over the attic. Megan and Jake were fingerprinted to eliminate their prints from any others they might find in the house. Detective Yarborough took their statement and asked questions for what seemed like forever. The detective was inclined to put it down as just a robbery in which Jake got in the way.

Megan and Jake knew there was more to it, but their story sounded so fantastic that the detective thought they were nuts or making it all up. Ghosts and riddles were not what he usually dealt with.

Detective Yarborough was also called when Megan's grandmother had been found at the bottom of the stairs. He had declared it an accident and hadn't investigated it any further. The police had no reason to consider foul play.

"We'll look over what we have at the station. I'll get back to you if we have anything to work with," the detective said, following the forensic team out of the house.

After they were gone, Jake and Megan got their second cup of coffee. It was now going on ten, and it was time to see Clarissa. Megan washed up the few dishes, and Jake fed Fur Ball and made sure the back door was securely locked. Just before going out, Jake got a call from his agent in Boston. The call was short, and soon they were on their way.

As they walked out to the car, Jake told Megan what his agent had to say. "It looks like we might have a little more money for the wedding. My latest book just made the Times' bestseller list. I might have to do some book signings, but I talked William—William Edwards, that's my agent—into holding off scheduling anything for a bit," Jake said, opening the car door for Megan.

"Wow, that's great!" said Megan.

"Congratulations! Are all your books bestsellers?"

"Some are," he said. "Women like my characterizations and romantic intrigue, and guys like the action and suspense. I have faithful fans that are always eager to read my upcoming stories and buy them as soon as they hit the market."

*****

They took Jake's Mercedes to the Salem Museum. The receptionist, whose nametag said "Jane Galloway," greeted them politely. She was the same volunteer they had talked with the last time they were there. She appeared to be in her late forties, with strawberry blonde hair piled on her head in a loose bun. Jane was the exact opposite of the flamboyant Clarissa. She wore a long cranberry wool skirt, with a matching cranberry cardigan sweater hung shapelessly over a buttoned-up white blouse. The only jewelry she wore was a Gaelic brooch at her neck.

Megan asked if Clarissa was in yet.

"Yes, she's here. I saw the light was on in her office when I came in. She usually doesn't come in until just about ten but must have had something pressing to do. I'll see if she's still busy," she said. She walked over to Clarissa's office and knocked on the door.

There was no answer.

"Clarissa, have you got those headphones on again?" Jane asked as she turned the doorknob and opened the door. Jane screamed. "Clarissa! Clarissa! Are you all right?"

Megan and Jake pushed their way into the room beside Jane, who tried to get a response from Clarissa. Clarissa's head was down on her desk like she had just dozed off.

"I don't think she's going to answer you, Jane," said Jake, after checking Clarissa's carotid artery for a pulse. "I'm sorry, but she's gone."

He turned to embrace Megan. She was in shock and starting to cry softly.

"Jane, I think you'd better go call the police," he said.

Jake guided both women out of the office. Jane called the police, and the three of them took seats in the reception area to wait. Jake immediately thought the worst—that Clarissa had been murdered because she knew something important. There were too many unanswered questions, especially after the events of last night. He didn't want to upset Megan or Jane with his theory until the police had a chance to look at the situation.

"Jane, you said the light was on in Clarissa's office when you came in this morning. Did you talk to Clarissa today?" Jake asked.

"I came in and called to her, letting her know I was here and started a pot of coffee. She didn't answer, but that's not unusual, as, I said, she sometimes has her headphones on. I was just checking my emails and was about to bring her some coffee when you came in."

"Could she have had any visitors before you came in this morning?" he asked.

"No, I don't think so. Hmm, I just remembered something. I didn't have to use my key to get in the door. That's odd because Clarissa leaves it locked if she gets here first. We don't unlock the door until ten. I didn't think of that until now. I locked it on my way out last night because Clarissa was still here. She said she just had a couple more things to look up before she called it a night," Jane said, speaking slowly, making sure to get it right.

Jake decided to keep his theory to himself for now. No point in scaring anyone without cause.

"I'm sorry, Jane," he said. "She might have had a heart attack or something. We'll just have to wait and see."

Megan found a box of tissues and handed them to Jane. Both women cried softly.

The police showed up a half-hour later. Detective Yarborough was not pleased to see Jake and Megan again. "Trouble just seems to follow you two around, doesn't it?" he asked. He sent the coroner's team into Clarissa's office and told Megan, Jake, and Jane, "Please stay where you are until I see what's what. I'd appreciate it."

"I don't think he likes us very much," Megan said, sitting close to Jake and holding both his hand and Jane's.

"I don't think he likes anyone," Jane said. "Clarissa told me he gave her a hard time about Corey's death. He told Clarissa just to accept her death as an accident and stop with all the wild theories. I can't believe she's dead now, too."

The detective came out a few minutes later. The coroner sent someone out to get a gurney for Clarissa's body and started packing up the scene.

"Well, it looks like a straightforward heart attack. There are no visible wounds on the body, so I think we can rule out foul play for now," the coroner said.

"Can you please tell me what you two were doing here this morning? Didn't you have enough excitement last night?" Detective Yarborough asked Megan and Jake.

"We came to talk to Clarissa about what had happened last night. We wanted to know who might be aware of that back way to the attic. I didn't even know it was there," Megan said, finding her voice again. She was getting mad that the detective didn't believe them and was not even trying to have an open mind.

"Why would Clarissa know anything about something like that?" the detective asked.

"History was her specialty, and it is a historic house," said Jake. "She knows—well, knew—about the history and the architecture of the houses in the area." He was upset with the detective's attitude, too.

"I don't expect any surprises with the autopsy, but if I have any more questions for any of you, I'll be in touch." Turning to Megan and Jake, he said gruffly, "I don't want you two playing amateur detective and making something out of nothing. Do I make myself clear?"

After he asked Jane the same questions Jake did, he folded up his little notebook and stuffed it in his jacket pocket.

"Jane, I'm sorry for your loss," he said and walked out the door.

Megan started to cry again. Clarissa was her friend, too. They had not known each other long, but she liked her and the connection she had with her grandmother. Jake hugged her and handed her another tissue from the almost- empty box.

"Jane, if there's anything we can do to help, please let us know. Did Clarissa have any family members who need to be notified?" Jake asked.

"Yes, she had a sister in Barnstable and a brother in Natick, I think," said Jane. "The numbers should be in the phonebook on her desk. I can call them and let them know. She was well-liked and well-respected in the community. She had a wonderful knowledge of the area's history. I can't quite get my head around all this."

She sniffled. "Jake and Megan, thank you so much for being here. This is dreadful. Clarissa never complained of being ill or having any problems, and we did share a lot, working so close together."

"Are you going to be alright now? Do you want us to stay a bit with you?" offered Megan, who had regained her composure.

"No, dear, I'll be fine. I'm going to close the office today and get on with things. I have to make those phone calls to Clarissa's family and notify the director of the historical society," Jane said with a sigh.

"Okay. Let us know about the arrangements and if the police get back in touch about anything," said Jake.

"Call if you need anything," Megan said, hugging Jane.

"Don't worry. I will."

Chapter 19

Once they were seated in the car, Megan took a deep breath. "Well, what do you think? Is it a coincidence, or do you think she could have been killed because she knew something?" Megan asked.

"I don't know what to think. If it turns out Clarissa was murdered, someone just upped the stakes," Jake said as he turned on the engine and headed for home.

As they pulled into the driveway, they saw Zack putting up Halloween decorations next door in his front yard. There were gravestones all over the grass. Zombies crawled out of some of the graves; decaying hands reached up out of others. White spider webs decorating some of the gravestones created an eerie effect. Zack was busy trying to untangle a string of orange lights to put on the bushes near the house. Full-size zombies, vampires, and other creepy creatures were lying about waiting to be put up somewhere.

"Hey, want to lend a hand?" Zack waved a fake, bloody arm in the air and laughed.

Jake and Megan, arm in arm, crossed over to Zack's house.

"Hi, Zack. Can we talk inside for a few minutes?" Jake asked.

"Sure. Amanda's at the gallery getting set up for the opening tomorrow night. We got some great stuff from that guy in Derry. I'm going out later tonight to finish up. So what's with all the cops at your house this morning?"

They followed Zack into the house, which was also getting the Halloween treatment. Zack decorated the outside with all his creepy zombies and vampires, but Amanda had gone with a witch-and-black-cat theme. She had draped swags of silk fall leaves at the windows and along the fireplace mantel. A black cauldron filled with blood-red chrysanthemums sat on the table in the dining room. She had placed pumpkin planters containing colorful fall leaves and flowers here and there.

"This looks like a picture in a magazine. It's so stunning!" said Megan. "Amanda has an artistic eye."

"She sure does. Here you go—grab a seat. Would you like to have some coffee?" Zack offered, very curious to know what was going on.

"No, thanks, but we do have some news for you," Megan said.

"Yeah, tell me about all those cops this morning. I was going to come over to see what had happened, but your car was gone by the time I got my act together."

"We had an intruder last night," said Jake. "He was up in the attic making noise and woke Megan up. I went up to check it out, but he got away. We called the cops out this morning to let them know," Jake said.

"That's not all of it," Megan said. "Jake got shot at. He's lucky to be alive. Didn't you hear the gunshots last night?" She figured the whole of Salem should have heard it. It sounded so loud in the house.

"What? Amanda is going to go nuts. She wasn't here to hear this! We're both very heavy sleepers, so not much can wake us up." Zack was almost bouncing in his chair with excitement.

"When Megan woke me, I heard a noise in the attic like someone moving stuff around. I got my gun out."

"Wait, you have a gun?" Zack asked."He has a big pistol," Megan said.

"Really? Can I see it sometime?" Zack asked, sounding as excited as a kid.

"Never mind the gun for now. Can I tell the rest of the story?" Jake asked. "When I got to the attic, I saw someone rummaging in an old trunk up there. Fur Ball picked just that moment to notice me and meow as he came to me on the stairs. The intruder saw me and fired at me. I tried to fire back, but that darn cat was wrapped around my legs and threw me off balance. By the time I untangled myself, the person was gone. He didn't pass by me, though, so I went looking and found a back stairway leading down to Megan's grandmother's bedroom off the kitchen."

"Can you believe it?" asked Megan. "I never even knew there was a stairway there, and I don't know if my gran did, either."

"You just never know about these old houses, do you? What did the police have to say?" asked Zack.

"It was a Detective Yarborough who came out," said Megan. "He's the same one who investigated when Gran died if you can call that an investigation. Yarborough said last night was probably a robbery attempt and blew it off. He wouldn't listen to anything we said to him."

Megan cleared her throat. "There's more," she said. "Remember we talked about Clarissa from the historical society? You might have met her at the house after the funeral—she was dressed in very elaborate colors. Anyway, she was Gran's friend and was trying to help us. Well, she's dead." Megan got all misty-eyed again.

"What? How? When?" asked Zack. "Amanda is going to flip when she finds out that she missed all this."

"We went to her office this morning to ask if anyone might have known about the back stairway to the attic. You know, like maybe it was a common style element in these old houses," Megan said. "Her assistant, Jane, went to tell her we were there and found her at her desk, dead. That dreadful Detective Yarborough came out again. He asked a few questions, said it looked like a heart attack, and left."

"Jane said she'd let us know if there's any news," said Jake. "The detective said if it turns out it was something other than a heart attack, he'll call. I'd love to know what Clarissa was working on that kept her there late last night."

"Now, about all that stuff on your front lawn, do you need any help with that?" Jake changed the subject.

"As a matter of fact, yes, I could use some help. Could you test and straighten out the lights? I didn't put them away right last fall, and they're all tangled. I should know better—this happens every year! I have a couple of strings of blinking eyeballs and a cool smoke machine to hook up. The neighbor kids at our old house used to love that." Zack got up and rubbed his hands together, just thinking about it. He was like a big kid himself.

"I'll go and tidy up a bit. The police left fingerprint dust over everything. How about I make some lunch for all of us? Will Amanda be home soon?" asked Megan.

"Not until about five. Amanda will close up the gallery, and then I'll go there after we have dinner."

"I'll see you later then. I'll call you two boys in for lunch." Megan giggled on her way out the door.

"Zack, let's go untangle these lights of yours," said Jake, following Megan out the door. Zack grabbed his old canvas hat off the peg by the door and crammed it on his head.

"Hey, Jake, I'm setting up some eerie sound effects, too. Don't you just love Halloween?" Zack asked as he skipped out the door.

Jake's cell phone rang. It was William again. He talked to him a few minutes about rescheduling his book signings, and then he started helping Zack with the lights, eyeballs, and zombies. He was happy to have the diversion, especially since Halloween was one of his favorite holidays, too. He was looking particularly forward to it this year, for one special reason.

Chapter 20

Megan cleaned off fingerprint dust for the next hour. She made up some ham sandwiches and a jug of iced tea and called the guys in for lunch. She was thrilled that Zack and Jake were getting on so well together. They all sat around the kitchen table discussing the break-in and Clarissa's death, tossing around different theories.

Zack went back to work on his display after lunch. He couldn't wait to tell Amanda all about what Megan and Jake had told him.

Jake and Megan sat together on the couch, holding each other. Megan rested her head on Jake's shoulder. "Jake, what do you think is going on around here?" she asked.

"I was wondering about that while I was helping Zack," Jake said. "I think it's connected with the treasure that's supposed to be hidden here in the house. Someone's looking for it or clues to its whereabouts.

"When you talked to Prendergast about selling, whoever was looking got nervous that time was running out. If you sell to Prendergast, he might just pull the old house down, and the treasure would be lost forever.

"I've also been thinking that whoever it is might be afraid that you would find it before they did. It's like one of my mystery novels. There's a cast of characters, and we need to find out more about each of them."

"What about Kathy at the Dockside? She knows almost everybody. I'll bet she could help. Let's have lunch there tomorrow and see if she'll talk to us," Megan said.

"Good thought. But for now, how about we go upstairs and catch up on some of that sleep we missed last night?" Jake said.

"I'm too upset to sleep right now. My head is just reeling with all that's happened," Megan replied.

"Well, if you can't sleep, I can think of something to help you relax. How about a nice back rub—or maybe there are other parts you would like rubbed?" Jake asked, flashing that quirky grin of his.

"You know, now that you mention it, a back rub or something might be just what I need right now." Megan took Jake's hand and tugged him toward the stairs. "Come on and show me just how good your back rubs are."

After a bit of back rubbing and other things, they did fall asleep for a while until Fur Ball woke them by purring and butting their faces. "Think he's hungry?" asked Jake, stretching his six-foot-six frame. What time is it?"

"It's almost six, no wonder the poor thing is hungry. I haven't had an afternoon nap like that in ages. The 'awake' part was pretty good, too," Megan smiled.

"Only pretty good? Well, practice makes perfect, and I do like to practice with you," Jake said, making a grab for Megan as she slipped out the other side of the bed.

"Oh, no, you don't! I'm starving. So is Fur Ball. How about making us an omelet and a salad?"

"How about we shower and then think about that omelet?" Jake asked, picking Megan up and carrying her to the shower.

*****

Dinner was a bit late that night, and they all had good appetites—even Fur Ball, who had to wait for his supper as well.

Megan and Jake were cuddling on the couch in front of the fire and watching an old movie on the television. Both lost in their thoughts about the past days' events when the quiet was interrupted by Jake's cell phone ringing.

"It's Amanda," said Jake, glancing at the name on the screen. "Hi, Amanda." Jake listened for a minute and then said, "No, he's not here." Jake was quiet. "Do you want us to go with you?" he asked. "Okay, we'll be right over."

"What's going on?" Megan asked after Jake ended the call.

"Grab your jacket," said Jake, picking up his car keys. "Amanda expected Zack home about an hour ago, and he's not answering his cell or the gallery phone. He has their car, so she asked us to take her to the gallery in case there's something wrong."

"Let's go. I hope Zack's phone battery died, or he forgot the time. I could see him doing something like that." Megan didn't want to think of other possibilities.

They picked up Amanda and rushed to the Longstreet Gallery. Amanda fretted the whole way. She worried that there was something wrong one minute and threatened to kill Zack herself if nothing was. When they got there, the lights were all on, and the door was unlocked.

"Zack never leaves the door unlocked when he's by himself and the gallery is closed," said Amanda. "He was just supposed to check the hanging of the work and come right home."

"Let me go first," Jake said, taking out his Glock.

"Why in heaven's name did you bring that?" asked Megan.

"After last night and this morning, I'm not taking any chances," Jake replied.

"Zack! Zack! Where are you? You'd better answer me!" Amanda called, her voice shaking with fear.

A groan came from the back of the gallery. "Oh, my God!" cried Amanda racing to look for Zack.

They found him lying in the storage closet. He had a large gash on his head that gushed blood. Amanda plopped down on the floor and cradled Zack's head on her lap. Megan ran to get a towel to stop the bleeding, and Jake dialed 911.

*****

A dark figure watched from a shadowy doorway across the street. He had picked the backdoor lock quickly, slipped in, and made his way around the gallery. He hadn't worried about making noise because no one was supposed to be there.

What he was looking for was not on the wall where he was told it would be, so he decided to snoop some more. Just as he started to rummage in a storage closet in one of the back rooms, he heard someone call out. The information he had been given was wrong. The gallery was supposed to be empty tonight.

She'll be furious I messed up again. The man darted away. He didn't want to have to explain his presence in the area that night.

Chapter 21

"Here we go again. Detective Yarborough will not be happy to see us," Megan groaned.

"He'll just have to suck it up and admit something is going on here," Jake said.

"But why the gallery?" asked Amanda, clearly upset. "What could they possibly want here? We don't carry anything that valuable. We only carry local art by local artists. I just don't understand any of this."

"Ow! I'm going to have one hell of a headache," said Zack. "Thanks, guys, for coming to my rescue." Zack reached up and drew Amanda down to give her a tender kiss.

Zack sat up slowly and held the towel to his head.

"Don't get up yet," Amanda cautioned. "Wait for the paramedics, please. You need to be checked out, and I think you might need x-rays and a few stitches."

Jake was starting to feel that he knew what the intruder was after; if it was one of his mystery novels, that's how he would write it.

"I think they were after the painting of the Lady in Green," he said. "Somehow, they know there's a connection between that painting and the mysterious treasure. They thought the painting was still here and came looking for it. Zack wasn't supposed to be here and got in the way like I did last night."

"At least he only conked me on the head and didn't shoot at me," Zack said.

"Oh, my God, I didn't think of that. My poor baby, you could have been killed!" Amanda grabbed Zack fiercely and hugged him tightly.

"Ow! Easy, Amanda, I'm a wounded man here." Zack winced.

"Sorry," she said, releasing her tight hug.

Just then, the flashing lights of the police cruiser and ambulance danced through the gallery windows. Jake went to let them in the door.

"Oh, crap," said Megan when she saw Detective Yarborough striding toward them.

"I should have guessed," he said. "It's been one thing after another since you arrived in town."

"It's not me," said Megan. "I tried to tell you something's going on, but you won't listen. It started with my gran being killed, and it's not over yet."

I still think your grandmother just had a terrible accident," said the detective. "It's not unusual for older people to fall, especially on stairs. I don't see how her death could be connected to a break-in here at the gallery. I think it's much more suspicious that you two show up every time there's trouble here in Salem."

"Detective Yarborough, we are not the bad guys here," said Jake. "You have got to listen to us. Someone killed Megan's grandmother.

Someone was in her house and shot at me. Someone killed Clarissa, and someone hit Zack over the head."

"All I want to deal with right now is what happened here tonight. The only voice I want to hear is Mr. Longstreet's. Am I making myself clear?"

Zack went over his evening step by step. He had arrived around seven and was just going to check the artwork's placement for the upcoming opening. Zack went to his office and answered emails when he heard someone moving things around in the storage closet. He thought it might be Amanda, so he called out her name, but then remembered he had the car so that it couldn't be her.

Whoever it was had heard him call out and stopped making noise. Zack admitted it was foolish, but he went to check, anyway. As soon as he stepped into the closet, he was hit from behind and went out like a light.

A police officer came in and spoke to Yarborough.

"Our officers have found the back door's been forced," the detective told them. "We'll have the forensic team dust for fingerprints, but I don't expect to find any. Crooks are getting smarter, thanks to the CSI programs."

The ambulance took Zack to the hospital to get checked out, and Amanda rode with him. She promised to call for a ride home when they were done. They could pick up their car from the gallery later.

"Look, you two," said Detective Yarborough. "Maybe it's just coincidence, but you need to leave it to the police. Don't go poking around. Next time he might not miss his target."

The detective followed his men out, reminding Jake and Megan not to touch anything before the forensic team had a chance to look around.

"That man is someone else I don't trust," Megan said. She hesitated before adding, "Either he's just too old school and has to have proof in his hands, or . . . could he possibly be in on it? He keeps dismissing our ideas. He won't even consider that all these things could be connected. He would be the perfect person to deflect suspicion."

"Let's give him the benefit of the doubt for now," said Jake. "Maybe he's starting to put the pieces together and realizes there's a lot more to this than just random accidents and break-ins. And you know what? If whoever broke in here didn't find whatever they were looking for, they might try our house again. I'm willing to bet it's that painting and the riddle on the back they're looking for. But I can't figure out who it might be. We better get back in case he's not done for the night."

Jake put his arms around Megan's waist and pulled her close. "Don't worry; we'll get to the bottom of this."

*****

They rode home in silence, lost in their thoughts. Jake wanted to believe the detective would do his job and wrap this all up, like in his mystery stories. Megan was afraid. She found it hard to trust the detective.

Fur Ball greeted them at the front door when they got home, purring and rubbing up against their legs. They had given up trying to contain the little cat. Megan picked him up and snuggled his fur. "Come on, Trouble. Let's get you something to eat," she said.

Megan got out a tin of cat tuna and a few Friskies and put them down for Fur Ball. She poured two glasses of wine and took them to the sitting room while Jake took a look around the house to make sure everything was as they had left it.

Jake got the fire going again, and they talked again about the events of the last couple of days.

"I wish the lady in the painting could talk and tell us what is going on," Jake said. "We don't even know what the treasure is or if there is one. Whoever is doing this could be all wrong. There might not be any treasure at all."

A little after midnight, Amanda called for a ride home. Zack was fine. He had a few stitches and a great scar to talk about. He was going to have a whopper of a headache, and Amanda would have to watch him for a day or two.

Chapter 22

In the morning, Megan and Jake sat at the breakfast table. Fur Ball was in his usual place on Jake's lap. Jake spoiled him by feeding him bits of bacon or sausage from his plate. If he did not feed him fast enough, he would sneak his little black paw onto Jake's plate and see what he could snag.

"I love mornings with you," said Jake, as he watched Megan get up and start to clear up the dishes. Megan wore the top of a set of Jake's pajamas, while Jake wore the bottoms.

"You can stop leering at my backside any time now!" She laughed, filling the sink with hot, soapy water.

"It's my favorite view in the morning."

"That's enough about my bottom for a while," said Megan, watching Jake sneak Fur Ball another tidbit. "Would you please stop feeding that cat at the table? He's spoiled enough."

"I think we'd better go see Kathy at the Dockside today," said Jake, changing the subject. "We can go over who might have known about the backstairs for one thing and also who might know the history of the house and the so-called treasure."

"I agree. Kathy's knowledge about the locals and who-does-what should be a big help."

"Have you spoken to Amanda about moving the Halloween party to this house yet?" Jake asked. "It's only a week away."

"I did, and at first, I could tell she was disappointed not to have it at her house. But then, after thinking about having the opening to worry about, she decided that it might be a good idea after all. And it's only one house away. She even said she would help to decorate it a bit.

I suggested that the party start at her house with drinks and nibbles and then move here for a buffet. She thought that was a great idea. She gets a party, and we get a wedding. Before you ask, I didn't tell her why we wanted to have some of the party here. It's still a deep, dark secret.

"Speaking of the wedding," Megan continued, "I want to order some flowers for decoration and a small bouquet to carry. We'll also need to order a cake, and I should call the caterers and housecleaners, too. On second thought, can we see Kathy tomorrow? I need to make these phone calls, and I'm really tired from the last couple of nights."

"No problem. I need to call my agent as well. With the new book coming out soon, I want to check what signings and other events he's lining up. I have something else to check on, too. We can stay home today and take care of things—and maybe get in a little nap this afternoon." Jake had that twinkle in his eye that said he had something else on his mind.

"I know your idea of an afternoon nap, and it doesn't involve sleeping." Megan was very happy and content with Jake. All her other problems could disappear for a while.

After making their phone calls, Megan realized she was getting excited about their future. The wedding was coming together: The florist was bringing some fall flowers for the mantel and arrangements for the tables; the caterers were providing a simple buffet and drinks, and the cleaners would come out the day before the ceremony.

They talked about taking a drive to Boston one day soon so Megan could shop for a dress for the wedding. She didn't want the big white-dress-and-veil thing and wanted a simple, long dress, maybe with a jacket. She didn't want white, maybe a cream or ivory. She'd know the right one when she saw it.

She got a bit tearful when it hit her that neither her parents, Gran or Clarissa, would be there. Jake guessed what she was thinking and held her tight. "It's going to be okay. I know you miss your family and Clarissa. They'll be there, looking down and feeling happy for you."

"I love you, Jake."

"I love you, too. Now—how about that nap?" Jake lifted Megan and slung her over his shoulder, and carried her up the stairs.

*****

The next day they drove to the Dockside Café to see if they could talk with Kathy and see what she might know about Salem residents that might be involved in what was happening.

Kathy was busy serving, but it was getting a bit slower after the morning rush. They chose a quiet table in the back and waited for Kathy to come over.

"Hi, folks! What can I get you to drink while you look at the menu?" she asked in her cheery voice.

"Just coffee, for now, Kathy," said Megan. "Kathy, do you remember us from the other day? You knew my gran, and we had a little chat.

"Oh, yeah, now I do. I see so many people. How's it going? You have the old house up for sale yet?"

"No, not yet. I'm still undecided. Do you have a few minutes to talk? We were hoping you might be able to help us with something," Megan asked.

"Sure. Just give me a few minutes to catch up. I'm due for a break. I'll be back." Kathy left to tend to the couple of customers that were left from the morning.

After Kathy walked away, Jake said, "We'll ask her to fill us in on some people. We don't have to tell her why. Okay?"

"We don't know a lot about her, either, so we have to be careful. I get it," answered Megan, just as Kathy returned.

"Mind if I sit for a bit? My feet are already killing me." Kathy eased herself into a chair where she could see if people in the restaurant needed her for anything. "Ahh, that's better," Kathy said, flexing her feet and ankles. "Now, what can I help you with?"

"Well, we don't know much about the people here and thought you might be able to fill us in a bit, like Mr. Prendergast, the real estate guy.

What's his story?" Jake asked. He'd start with a couple of normal questions for someone trying to sell a house.

"That guy? He comes in a bit. He likes the meatloaf and is a lousy tipper. He's a bit creepy, but I think he's pretty harmless. I've heard he's very fair with the people he buys houses from and does a good job with his condos, too. I know a few people that have bought them, and they don't have any complaints that I know of. He's been around a couple of years now. He's not the chatty type when he's here alone. Sometimes he'll bring in a potential customer, and then it's all business talk," Kathy said. "Anyone else you want to know about?"

"Yea, what about that lawyer Halloran and his secretary, Julia Parrish?" Megan asked. "He's pretty dressy for a Salem lawyer working out of a small, second-floor walkup."

"Oh, he's great. He grew up here in Salem but has a big office in Boston. He splits his time between there and here and does a lot of free work for the older residents like your grandmother or others he knows don't have a lot of money. Sometimes he charges only what he has to and not for his time. He's a pretty important lawyer in Boston, and I guess he likes to give back to his hometown," Kathy said.

"He comes in once in a while with Miss Parrish. I don't care for her very much. She's fussy about her food, can't have this, and doesn't like that. Mr. Halloran, now, he likes our pies. Mr.Halloran always has a chat, just about the weather or local stuff, very friendly. Miss Parrish, she's a different kettle of fish. —but not her. She never has a dessert. She never talks except to complain or tell me how she wants her food prepared. I get the feeling she thinks she's better than me and likes putting me in my place. If she's here alone, I let one of the other servers deal with her. She's a right pain in the butt if you ask me," Kathy huffed.

"Wow, I guess you don't like her very much! Does she have relatives here? Maybe she grew up privileged or something," Megan said, trying to coax more out of Kathy.

"I think I heard she grew up pretty poor. Her family left Salem when she was in her teens. She might have a couple of cousins left around. I was surprised when she came back and started to work for Mr. Halloran. I knew her from school, but she was a grade or two above me, and Halloran was a grade or two above that."

Just then, Jake's cell phone rang. He looked at the caller's name. "It's Detective Yarborough," he said as he took the call. "Detective, what can I do for you? We don't have any dead bodies for you today."

Jake listened to the detective for a few minutes before ending the call.

"You'll never guess what he just told me. The autopsy on Clarissa came back. We'd better go."

To Kathy, he said, "Thanks very much, Kathy. If we have more questions, may we come back?"

"Sure, I don't mind. It's kind of fun. You suspect something, don't you? I looked you up. I knew I'd seen you before. I have one of your books, Mr. Durant. You're a mystery writer. Are you going to write a book about it? Can I be in it if you do? Can you make me sultry and sexy, please?" Kathy was excited. She knew it; there was a real, live mystery right under her nose, and she was helping to solve it.

Megan and Jake got in his Mercedes and left the Dockside parking lot. "What's up, Jake? What did Detective Yarborough have to say?"

"He wants us at the police station, said he's ready to listen to us now. Something must have turned up in the autopsy to change his mind," Jake told Megan.

Chapter 23

They drove the few blocks to the station, which was in one of the older buildings in Salem, and smelled of coffee and sweat. They checked in with the desk sergeant, and he immediately escorted them upstairs to the detective's office.

"Thanks for coming so quickly. Have a seat," Yarborough said, indicating a couple of chairs in front of his cluttered desk. "There was a surprise for me in the autopsy. I'm sorry for not giving what you were saying more credence. I'm afraid Clarissa McDowell was murdered."

He paused to let that statement sink in. "The pathologist found a small needle mark just below her right ear. He thinks she was injected with an insulin needle filled with air. It was so tiny he almost missed the site, but a slight bruise showed up after the postmortem examination. The air in the needle would have created an air embolism, and that would make it look like Miss McDowell had a heart attack."

Yarborough looked at Megan. "Since now it appears she was killed, we have to revisit the death of your grandmother and also the break-ins at the gallery and your house. It took me a while, but I do believe now that all these events are connected somehow. Please tell me all you know and all you think you know about what might be going on here." He sat back in his chair and got out a new, clean notebook. "I'm ready to listen."

Megan and Jake took turns filling him in on what they suspected. Megan told him about her recent, strange conversations with Clarissa about her grandmother's sense that someone was in the house. Megan recalled the phone call she'd had with her gran the day she died. She told him Gran cut it short because she had heard something.

Jake described the night of the break-in at their house. The detective already had Zack's statement about the night at the gallery.

Megan looked at Jake, who gave a nod for her to tell about the rumors.

She took a deep breath and began. "There have been rumors about a treasure associated with the house. We think the person responsible for all of this is looking for the treasure or clues to where it might be."

Megan held out her hand. "My grandmother left me this ring. She left me a rather strange message with it. In the message, she said to always wear the green for special occasions. We have no idea what that could mean."

"There was a portrait in the Longstreet Gallery called 'The Lady in Green,'" said Jake. "The person in the painting is the spitting image of Megan."

"Sorry. What do you mean, was in the gallery?" asked the detective.

"Zack and Amanda gave it to Megan the night before the gallery break-in," continued Jake. "They figured it must belong to her family. Maybe the lady was a distant relative."

"On the back of the painting, there was another riddle," Megan said. "Maybe this person found out about the painting and about the riddle being a clue and went to the gallery looking for it. I wonder how they found out, and, more importantly, who found it out?" said Megan.

"Also, why are they so certain the rumor is true?" asked Jake.

"Okay, now I see why you thought there was more to this, but we still don't have much to go on. Miss McDowell was murdered, and some events may or may not be related. We need proof. We still don't have any suspects. I suggest you two go home and stay out of trouble. I'll do some digging and let you know if I find anything." Detective Yarborough closed his notebook and stood up to send Megan and Jake on their way.

*****

They walked down the station stairs and out to the parking lot. It was a relief to get out of the old, claustrophobic building. Not many leaves still clung to the trees now. The days were feeling damp, and the nights were beginning to darken earlier and earlier. The street lights would be coming on soon.

"We need to talk to Jane at the museum. Clarissa might have left something on her desk that she was working on. Maybe she found out something that got her killed," Jake said to Megan over the roof of his car as he opened the car door.

"I think you may be right," Megan agreed. "But who would have known about what she found? I just don't understand." They got in the car and drove a couple of short blocks to the Salem Museum.

The lights were on in the building when they arrived.

"Well, someone is here at least," Megan said, getting out of the car.

Jane was sitting at her desk, typing.

"Hi, how are you two doing? Detective Yarborough called and told me about what they found out in the autopsy. I just can't believe Clarissa was murdered—and for what?"

"Jane, has anyone been in Clarissa's office since you found her?" Jake asked.

"No, just the police. Why?"

"We'd like to take a look at her desk. Maybe she was working on something. Did you check to see if anything was missing?"

"I haven't had a chance to look. She usually assigned me event notices and stuff like that. I wasn't a researcher like she was. Right now, I'm designing a notice about a memorial service for Clarissa to be held here. Julia Parrish, from Mr. Halloran's office, offered to help with anything I might need. It seems she's also into the history of Salem. I knew her and her cousin Frank from school before she moved away. We've kind of reconnected in the last few months."

The police would find this out, anyway, Jane thought.

"Jane, it might be important. May we look in her office, please?" Megan asked. She knew Jane and Clarissa must have been close. They had worked together for quite a few years.

"I guess it'll be alright. The police have finished in there." Jane was worried but thought, What could they find that the police hadn't found already?

Megan and Jake felt strange walking into the office, knowing what had happened there. Fingerprint dust was on the desk and the phone. Jake sat in Clarissa's chair and just looked at the paperwork there for a moment, without touching it. This was exactly how she had left it, and he wanted to get a sense of what she was doing. Most of it was lists of events and flyers for some upcoming Halloween ghost tours. Jake opened the desk drawers one by one and shuffled through the contents. In the bottom drawer, under a bunch of other folders, he found one with the name Corey on it.

"I think we have something," Megan said. She was looking through the file cabinets and pulled out a folder labeled "Bishop House."

"I've got something, too," Jake said, putting the folder he found on the desk.

"Why are these two folders still here? Why didn't whoever killed Clarissa take them?" asked Megan, sitting in a chair in front of the old desk.

"I don't know, but it's a good thing for us that they didn't. You look through yours, and I'll look through the one I found and see what we have."

"Jake, let's ask Jane if we can take them home. I don't want to be away from the house for too long, just in case they come back. I'm worried they might try to take the painting or go rummaging around again."

"Good idea. We can take our time then. I'm hungry, and it's getting late."

Jake took the folders, and together they approached Jane about taking them home.

"I don't know about that," said Jane. "They might belong to the historical society and shouldn't leave the building. I'm responsible for the office until they find a replacement for Clarissa. Maybe you should leave them and come back tomorrow and take your time going over them then."

"Jane, we need to look at these," Megan said. "I promise that we will get them back to you undamaged. If they do connect to what is going on, we'll call Detective Yarborough and let him take a look."

Jane tried again to protest but decided to let the folders go. After all, she would still know where they were.

Chapter 24

When they reached the house, there was a light on in one of the windows. Darkness was coming earlier each day now.

"Did you forget to turn off that light when we left this morning?" Megan asked.

"No, I made the rounds of all the doors and the rooms like I always do."

"You don't suppose Fur Ball is afraid of the dark and turned on the lights?" said Megan, trying not to sound as afraid as she was.

They made their way to the front door and found it unlocked.

"Here we go again," said Jake, taking out his gun.

"Do you think that's necessary?" asked Megan, taking hold of Jake's arm.

"What, you think Fur Ball turned on the lights and left the door open for us?"

"No, I just hate guns." Megan cringed.

Slowly they opened the door and entered the foyer. They could see the light spilling out of the room that held the painting. They crept down the hallway and cautiously peeked in and saw the portrait of the Lady in Green against the couch with the riddle side showing.

At that same moment, they heard a loud crash up in the attic. They raced up the stairs to the attic door. Jake signaled for Megan to be quiet and stay back behind him. He eased open the door and went cautiously up the stairs.

He prayed that the stairs would not creak and also wondered where Fur Ball was. He had almost gotten him killed last time, and the cat had not greeted them at the front door.

Another crash and the sound of wood splintering filled the attic. Jake could see someone trying to break the old trunk apart. Woodchips and the contents of the trunk were strewn all over the floor. The old trunk was solid oak, though, and holding up well to the assault.

"Stop right now!" yelled Jake.

The intruder did stop, throwing his crowbar at Jake's head. Jake ducked just in time and was tackled and shoved aside. Megan was not so lucky. She was pushed down the stairs as the thief ran by. Jake jumped up, but instead of running after him, he stopped to check on Megan. She had taken a rough ride down the stairs and was knocked out.

He heard the front door bang shut and knew the thief had escaped again.

He picked Megan up and carried her to their bedroom. After gently laying her down, he called Detective Yarborough. He had Yarborough's number on speed dial in his phone now. He knew the detective would not be pleased to hear from him again so soon.

Megan came to just as Jake was finishing a call.

"Don't try to get up," he told her. "You've had a nasty bump to your head. Do you hurt anywhere else?" Jake adjusted the cold towel he had put on her head. "The police and the ambulance will be here in a few minutes. I called

Amanda. She's going to come over and sit with you. Zack is coming, too."

"Jake, where's Fur Ball? I expected her to get in the middle of things as she did before. I'm worried that bastard did something to keep her quiet. Please look for her," Megan pleaded, tears escaping, thinking the worst.

He kissed her lightly and said, "Sure. You just stay put."

The doorbell rang as he reached the bottom of the stairs. It was Amanda and Zack, followed almost immediately by the police.

"Glad you could come over. Amanda, can you go up and stay with Megan? She got a bit roughed up. There should be an ambulance coming to check her out. Zack, can you take a look around for Fur Ball? Megan is worried about him because she didn't get in the way."

Jake glanced at the detective heading up the walkway. "By the look on Yarborough's face, I'm going to get my head handed to me," he said.

"Jake, you're driving me into early retirement. What happened this time? I saw the Longstreets here. Were they involved again?" asked the detective.

"Not this time. They're our friends and live next door. I called and asked them to come over."

"As long as they stay out of the way, that's fine." Yarborough's tone was anything but pleasant.

Jake took the detective back up to the attic. There were papers and bits of the wooden trunk scattered all over. Behind the battered trunk, they found the tire iron that had been used to rip into it.

"I'll get this fingerprinted, but I don't expect we'll find anything. Did he manage to take anything this time?"

"We never got a chance to study what was in the trunk. We knew there were old papers in there, but that's about all there was."

"How's Megan doing? You said she got tossed down the stairs?"

"She took a knock to the head and was out for a few minutes. She'll need to go to the hospital."

"I've seen enough up here. Let's go check on Megan," Yarborough said.

When they arrived in Megan's bedroom, she was sitting up with Fur Ball in her lap. Amanda and Zack were sitting on opposite sides of the bed.

"Zack found Fur Ball," Megan said. "He was shut up in the downstairs bathroom, poor thing. It must be the same guy because he knew enough to get her out of the way."

The cat was hungry but otherwise unhurt.

"Poor baby. Was that bad man mean to you?" she asked, cuddling the cat.

The ambulance arrived, and the paramedics started examining Megan. Amanda and Zack went down to the kitchen to wait for them to finish. They didn't know if Megan would need to go to the hospital or not. Amanda busied herself putting on a pot of coffee for everyone.

The paramedics followed the police down the stairs, and Jake showed the EMTs out. He explained to Amanda and Zack that Megan didn't seem to have any broken bones or internal injuries. She didn't need to go to the hospital, but they suggested Jake keep an eye on her and bring her in straight away if things changed.

Jake went into the sitting room to answer the detective's questions. They went over and over things. Yes, the door was locked when they left. There were no signs of forced entry. How did they get in? No, we didn't leave any lights on. Jake answered questions for a half-hour before Detective Yarborough was satisfied.

Chapter 25

Once he was gone, Jake went to help Megan downstairs and into a big, comfy, upholstered chair. He propped her feet up on a matching ottoman. Amanda put some ice in a towel for the lump on Megan's head and spread one of her gran's afghans over her knees.

"I'm not an invalid, you know. I only got a little bump on the head, for pity's sake. Stop fussing," she demanded. Fur Ball nestled snuggly on the soft afghan in her lap. Jake, concerned about Megan, sat on the arm of her chair.

Amanda passed around the cups of coffee, and they settled back to go over what had happened.

"What, no cookies?" Zack asked.

"There are no cookies, Zack. It's not our house with the magic cookie jar that never gets empty," Amanda said. "Sorry, folks, I spoil him with his sweets all the time. He's just a big kid at heart, but you gotta love him." Amanda said—giving his cheeks a tender pinch. "With all the sweets he eats, he should be as big as a house."

Jake got up and took the painting of the Lady in Green over to the light to read the riddle out loud again, "*The key to fortune can be found where friendship and togetherness hold your heart. Loyalty guards over all. The lock is in the branches of the tree where ancestors can be found. A symbol of a faraway past guards the green.*"

After letting the words sink in for a few moments, he said, "Let's break this down. Megan, you told me how that ring of yours should be worn. What else do you know about it? The riddles all seem to start with that." Jake was beginning to put something together in his head.

"Then there is the trunk. The intruder was trying to get into it, but we stopped him. What could the ring and the trunk have in common?"

Megan jumped up and sat down again fast as a wave of dizziness hit her. "Oh boy, I won't do that again in a hurry. When I had Zack come and check the house out that first time, I noticed the trunk and thought how quaint. There was lovely, intricate, Celtic carving about halfway down the side. The trunk held a bunch of old papers about the family genealogy. Where's Gran's note that came with the ring?"

Megan got up again, but a lot more slowly this time. She got her grandmother's note from the desk drawer and starting reading it to herself.

My dearest Megan,

I hope you like the gift I left for you. That ring was handed down to me by my mother, and by her mother, and so on, from mother to daughter through several generations. I hope you will wear it and enjoy the love of all the women who have worn it before you.

There are traditions to wearing the ring. When you're looking for love, the ring is worn on the right hand with the heart pointing away. When you find your love, the ring is moved to the left hand, the heart pointing in. There is magic in love, my dear. Enjoy it.

"Here's the part I think is important," Megan said, and she read the next bit out loud to the others.

There is an old trunk up in the attic that contains documents that trace the genealogy of the women that have worn the ring before you. Our line goes back to the Salem of old, all the way to the witch trials.

I have left you the old house and all it contains. It is yours to do with what you want. The house has stories to tell if you but look, and for a special occasion, always wear the green.

I love you, my darling,

Grandma Corey

"It's all about that old trunk," said Megan. "The riddle on the portrait of the Lady in Green is part of it. I'm sure of it. Jake, will you grab that painting, and let's go take a look at that old trunk."

The four of them made their way up to the attic. The space looked like a bomb had gone off. The old oak trunk had held up pretty well to the battering from the person trying to demolish it.

"Okay, 'the house has stories to tell if you but look,'" Megan read. She took a guess. "I think that's about the genealogy papers and records in the trunk. 'Always wear the green' might mean the ring, but I don't think so."

"Let me see the riddle on the painting," said Jake.

The group sat on the attic floor. Megan read the riddle, trying to figure out what it could mean. *"The key to fortune can be found where friendship and togetherness hold your heart—loyalty guards over all. The lock is in the branches of the tree where ancestors can be found. A symbol of a faraway past guards the green."*

"I have an idea," Jake said. "Look at the design on the trunk. Doesn't that carving look like branches of a tree?"

Megan ran her fingers over the intricate details on the front of the trunk.

"You're right; it does," she said. "And there's a shamrock, for Ireland, in the middle—a symbol of a faraway past."

Megan ran her fingers over the design again and stopped on the shamrock. It was loose and moved at her touch.

Amanda and Zack sat quietly, holding their breath.

Megan pushed on the shamrock a little harder, and it swung up to reveal a small keyhole.

"That's not shaped like any keyhole I've ever seen," said Amanda, pushing Zack out of her way to get a better look. "So, where's the key?" she asked.

"Megan, I think you're wearing it!" said Jake.

"I don't have any key, just my clothes and nothing in my pockets."

"The key is your ring. It said the key to fortune can be found where friendship and togetherness hold your heart.' Remember what your gran said about the symbols in the ring? Hand it here."

Megan gently slid the ring off her finger. Jake took the ring, twisting it to line up with the lock. He pressed it in and gave it a turn. It seemed as if all the air had left the attic as the tumblers clicked and a hidden drawer slid out.

"What is it? What is it? Is it the treasure?" Amanda demanded, again pushing Zack so she could see.

Zack pushed back. "I want to see, too," he said.

"Hold on. It's all wrapped up," Jake said. He lifted the package out of the trunk drawer, laid it on the floor, and motioned for Megan to do the honors of unwrapping it. "After all, it's yours."

Megan carefully took the wrappings off the package.

"Is it the treasure?" whispered Zack, trying to look over Amanda's shoulder.

As she peeled away the layers, Megan saw bits of green satin appear.

"It's the dress—the dress from the painting. It has to be. Is that the treasure?" Amanda was disappointed. She expected real treasure, like money or pirate booty.

Megan was not answering. Her eyes were closing, and she was drifting away again, slipping to the side, where Jake caught her in his arms.

"Megan! Megan, can you hear me?" Jake patted her face, trying to get her to come back.

"It's my wedding dress," Megan whispered. She shook her head, slowly coming back to the present. She sat up.

"What do you mean, 'my wedding dress?" asked Amanda.

"The dress in the portrait is her wedding dress," Megan said. She stood up and was going to hold the dress up in front of her when another smaller package tumbled out and hit the floor at Megan's feet. It was a small, green –velvet drawstring pouch. Jake reached it before she did. He held it out to her, but she was afraid to open it.

"I think I'd better sit down, just in case I try to pass out again."

She took the small pouch, untied the draw-string, and tipped the contents into her lap. There they saw the treasure glittering in the soft light of the attic—the necklace and earrings worn in the portrait by the Lady in Green. The emeralds had an inner fire that matched the solid gold of the setting.

A warm glow spread through Megan. It was a feeling of being loved and cherished. She saw and felt the necklace being put around her neck.

She felt a warm embrace encircle her and knew in her heart that the necklace was a symbol of undying love from the Lady in Green. She had to find out who she was and who had loved her so deeply.

"I don't know what to say. I'm speechless," said Amanda. "This is the treasure they have been looking for, and we found it." She picked up an earring and held it to her ear. "This is so beautiful."

"Maybe Megan will let you borrow it sometime," said Zack. "Of course, we'll have to have armed guards with us if you do."

Amanda giggled at the thought.

"We need to tell the police we found it, just to clear it with them," said Jake. "We should get it appraised and insured, maybe even put it in a safety deposit box. Thankfully our thief was not very clever at solving riddles."

"You're right," Megan said, still in shock over their find. "What do we do with it tonight? What if the intruder comes back?"

"Sleep with it under your pillow," Zack said. "Jake's got that big gun; he can protect you and the treasure at least until tomorrow morning."

"I think that's a good idea," said Jake. "Tomorrow, we can start to go through Clarissa's papers and see what got her killed."

"What about Jane? She'll want those papers back. What do we tell her?" Megan asked.

"We'll cross that bridge later," said Jake.

It was late, and Amanda and Zack had to open the gallery in the morning. Jake made them promise not to tell anyone about their discovery just yet.

"We still have a killer to find," he said.

Chapter 26

After breakfast the next morning, Jake called Detective Yarborough and filled him in. Next, he called a jewelry appraiser he knew in Boston.

Jake had contacted him for some information he needed for one of his novels. He was able to make an appointment for the next day.

Megan and Jake spent most of the weekend continuing to go through the contents of the house—particularly the papers they had found up in the old trunk. They managed to piece together a genealogy going back from Megan's grandmother to the early 1800s. Megan's great-great-grandmother was Lucinda Fitzgerald and had married Laurence Sinclair, a wealthy man in the shipping trade. There was a tax bill, dated 1854, for the house and land in his name. So they figured out that he had built the house for Lucinda.

The most amazing find was a June 1852 receipt for one gold-and-emerald necklace and earring set from a Boston jeweler. They finally knew who had bought the necklace and for whom.

Megan sat on the floor among all the papers, holding the receipt in her hands.

"He loved her so much," she said. "I'll bet she's the Lady in Green. I just know I'm right! But why did they hide it away as they did?"

"We need to keep digging, but let's stop and have some lunch first," Jake said. "Since we're going to Boston Monday, do you want to shop for your wedding outfit? The wedding is only next week, you know. We can have a nice dinner out or see a show. Wouldn't it be nice to get away from all this for a day?"

"I think a trip to Boston would be great, but I've already found my wedding dress. Our wedding is on Halloween, and I'm going to dress as the Lady in Green. Gran said, 'For a special occasion, always wear the green.'"

She set down the receipt and said, "I can't think of a more special occasion than getting married. I also want to see where you live. I want to get to know you in your own space, where you write, where you cook those wonderful meals. I want to see what you have hidden in your closets. Are you messy or neat? I want to sleep in your bed for a change."

"If that's what you want, then that's what will happen. Can I call my cleaning lady first and let her know we're coming?" Jake smiled and dialed the number.

*****

The next day, before leaving Salem, they dropped off Megan's wedding dress at a dry cleaner that specialized in bridal and evening apparel. The gown was in perfect condition but a bit musty after spending more than a century in the attic trunk.

They made good time getting to Boston and left Jake's car in the underground parking garage at his apartment building. They spent the next hour finding their way through the city on the subway. Since Jake was used to the Massachusetts Bay Transportation Authority and Megan was very accustomed to taking the subway in New York, it wasn't that difficult. It was just a bit scary knowing they were carrying some very expensive items around with them. Muggings and purse snatchings were common in the subways of Boston, like in any big city, as buskers and food vendors entertained, fed, and distracted the commuters traveling to and from the outlying areas.

Nevertheless, they traveled without incident, got off at the downtown Washington Street stop, and arrived early at the Jewelers Exchange Building for their appointment with the appraiser.

Mr. Friedman was a man average in height—who looked to be in his fifties, with gray hair and a beard, glasses perched on his nose, and a strong accent. He greeted them warmly and took them to his office.

"It's nice to see you again, Mr. Durant. I must say your phone call intrigued me. What have you got to show me?"

"I inherited some jewelry, and I need to know what I should insure it for," Megan said, taking the pouch out of her purse and placing it on the desk.

Mr. Friedman opened the pouch and turned the necklace and earrings out onto a piece of black velvet. After arranging the pieces, he placed a jeweler's loop against one eye and examined the emerald stones in the necklace.

"This is an incredible piece of jewelry," he said, unable to hide his interest and curiosity. "I have not seen workmanship of this quality in a long time. It is not a modern piece. Do you have any idea when it might have been created?"

"As far as we know, it was most likely made in the early1850's as a wedding gift for one of Megan's ancestors," Jake answered. There was no need to tell him how they found it.

"That makes sense. There is a mark that tells me who the maker was, but I would need to research it to find out about him, and the gold is stamped 22k, which is hardly used at all in the States now. The best we do is 18k. The smaller emeralds are about five carats each, and the single large one is ten. I love the proportions of the emeralds—not too small and not too large. I would say, to ensure the whole set, a value of close to $300,000 would be appropriate. If you wished to sell it, you could get double that at one of the big auction houses like Sotheby's."

He continued looking through the loop—admiring the pieces.

"I don't want to sell them," Megan said. "They mean a lot to me. They've been in the family this long, and I'm going to hang onto them."

"I'm glad to hear that," Mr. Friedman said. "So many people sell off the family jewels as soon as they can." He smiled. "I'll write you the appraisal form for the insurance company. It will only take a minute. You can have a look in the showroom while you wait. Maybe you can find something to add to your family's collection."

Jake and Megan took a look at the wonderful items in the display cases. In the end, they decided on a man's simple, gold Claddagh ring for Jake to receive at the wedding ceremony.

When they were finished, they made their way back to Jake's condo. It had been a while since he had been there, and some of his food had seen better days. After cleaning out his fridge and tossing out most of the contents, they took a walk down to Jake's favorite pub, Sullivan's, for something to eat.

Sullivan's was a true Boston Irish pub, not one of those sissy sports bars. The pub had dark wood floors, cozy booths, and a dartboard on one wall. Megan opted for some fish and chips, and Jake had shepherd's pie and a pint of Guinness. Arm in arm, they strolled slowly back to the condo. The autumn evening was damp, with a light fog coming in off the water.

Back at the condo, Megan did some snooping around and liked what she saw. Jake's place was a loft in the Back Bay, with a view of the harbor.

His writing desk was an orderly mess, and a number of his books, along with works by Patterson and Gresham, were stuffed in an over-flowing bookcase. A king-size bed dominated the bedroom, and they made good use of every inch of it that night.

Chapter 27

They made good time driving back to Salem in the morning since the traffic was all headed into Boston. Jake suggested they stop at the Dockside Café for a quick lunch. Kathy sat them in a booth with a view of Pickering Wharf. They had sandwiches and iced coffee and ordered clam chowder to go.

Jake noticed Jane sitting with Julia Parrish at a table in a back corner, deep in discussion.

"Get a load of that," he said to Megan as he nodded discreetly in their direction.

"I didn't know they knew each other that well," Megan whispered.

Kathy came back to leave the check.

"Kathy, can I ask you something?" Jake asked. "How often do Jane Galloway and Julia Parrish come in together?"

"Oh, they come in about once a week or so. It was right after Julia's mother died I started seeing them together. They seem pretty chummy."

Jake was tapping his fingers on the table, his brain starting to connect the dots. Were they the right dots? Or was it just the mystery writer in him?

"Kathy, we'd like to ask you to our house for Halloween if you're free," said Megan. "First, there will be drinks and nibbles next door at Zack and Amanda Longstreet's at seven, and then a buffet at our house at nine. We all hope you can come, and you can bring a date or a friend if you want."

Megan wrote out the address for Kathy.

"I haven't been to a Halloween party in ages. Do I get to dress up and wear a costume?" Kathy asked excitedly.

"Of course, wear a costume! We hope that most of the guests will," Megan answered. "Jake and I are dressing up and have a special surprise for everyone."

"Oh, I can't wait! Don't you just love Halloween?" Kathy asked as she hurried off to help other customers.

"Let's get back," Jake said. "Fur Ball hasn't figured out how to use the can opener yet." He had a soft spot for the little cat, even if Fur Ball had almost gotten him killed.

Megan was agreeable since she was still stiff and bruised from her tumble down the stairs and wanted a hot bath. On the way home, she was very quiet.

"What's on your mind? Are you getting cold feet?" Jake asked Megan.

"Not about the wedding. Don't worry about that," said Megan. "It's just that I was so sure of who I was and what I was doing in New York. It's all changed so fast. I've been in touch with Jennifer at the gallery, and they all want me back soon, but now I don't know if I want to go back. I like it here and who I am here, too. I've thought I might want to get back to painting and my career as an artist. I'm too busy to do that while I'm running the gallery. I have a choice to make, and it's difficult. That's all."

"It's okay, Megan. Whatever you choose, I'll be there for you. Remember, I can write anywhere."

*****

Almost before Megan turned the key in the front door, she felt that something was wrong. Jake felt it, too.

"Stay behind me," he said.

Megan was relieved when they walked in, and Fur Ball wrapped himself around their legs. Instead of the soft purr he usually greeted them with, he was meowing his head off. Jake picked him up and headed to the kitchen by way of the sitting room. It was a wreck.

All the desk drawers had been turned out, pillows were on the floor, and even the pictures on the wall had been moved. Clarissa's notes were scattered all around.

"Someone had a field day in here," said Jake. "Good thing we had the jewelry with us. They must have seen that the trunk had been opened and went looking for whatever we found."

"We have to find out who is doing this and fast," said Megan. "I'm tired of never knowing what I'll find when I open the front door."

"We'd better check the other rooms and see what state they're in."

"Should we bother Detective Yarborough?"

"Not this time. There's nothing he can do at this point. We know there won't be any prints. I'll head upstairs, and you can feed Fur Ball."

Jake made his way through the bedrooms on the second floor and found the same mess as downstairs. Up here, even the mattresses had been turned over. All the dressers' drawers had been pulled out, and their contents tossed all over the rooms.

He checked the attic and imagined the rage of the intruder upon finding the trunk empty. More damage had been done to the trunk. It looked like a tornado had been through the attic.

Jake came down and found Megan at the kitchen sink. She was holding onto the edge and just staring out the window to the back garden.

Even the kitchen drawers and cabinets had been searched. He came over and put his arms around her. She leaned back to relax against his solid chest for comfort. He gently kissed her neck.

"You're a mystery writer—can't you find an ending to all this? I'm scared, and I just want it all to stop!"

"It will stop. I promise you it will. We need to show whoever is doing this that we have the necklace and are not keeping it in the house but will be putting it in a safe deposit box. I just had an idea that might work to draw this lunatic out. We go around to all the people we know—Kathy at the diner, Jane at the historical society, your lawyer's office, and even that guy Prendergast. We tell them all that we have the jewelry and that you will wear it on Halloween night as part of your costume. We tell them that after the party, it goes to the bank for safekeeping."

"Okay, so I wear the necklace as bait for a murderer. Thanks a bunch for making me a target. Do you think it will work?"

"If I'm right, he'll try to steal it that night before it goes to the bank. I'm going to call Detective Yarborough and talk to him about the idea. He'll probably say we're nuts to try it, but we have to do something."

Jake squeezed Megan's hand. "I've also been thinking about how no one has ever seen anyone around the house," he said. "There's never a vehicle parked nearby that doesn't belong. Tomorrow we get busy and make plans to catch this guy."

"Jake, the house is a mess, and it's only a couple of days to Halloween. There's no way I can clean this up on my own while you play amateur sleuth. I'm calling the cleaning crew to see if they can come tomorrow instead of Halloween morning as I planned. Do you think we should tell Zack and Amanda our plans? They might be able to help."

"Just tell them the first part about dressing as the Lady in Green. We don't want to tip off anyone by accident," Jake cautioned. "I don't believe they're involved, but you never know who they might talk to."

Megan glanced around the room and sighed. "Let's just clean up the kitchen and our bedroom tonight," she said. "We can tackle the rest tomorrow and hope the cleaners can come early." She had had enough for one day. She wanted a hot bath and a good night's sleep without an intruder skulking around the house.

It didn't take long to put everything back where it belonged in the kitchen. They swept up broken glass from the floor, put fresh water down for Fur Ball, and changed his litter pan. When that was done, they climbed the stairs hand in hand, exhausted but ready to tackle the bedroom.

There was not a lot to pick up in the bedroom. Megan hadn't brought much with her, and Jake had only a change of clothes. While they were at his loft in Boston, he had added to his wardrobe and picked up a few other things, which were still in his case at the front door where he'd left them.

*****

After they finished straightening up, they shared a long, hot shower. The couple cuddled in Megan's old bed and talked about the future. Jake was honest with Megan and asked her to think about keeping the old house, suggesting that they turn it into bed and breakfast. He had a lot of ideas on how to renovate and repair the old place. He loved to cook and would also have time to write. She loved to paint and could use the room over the garage as a studio. She could also work with Zack and Amanda at their gallery.

"What about the gallery in New York?" Megan said. "It's been my whole life. I don't think I can give it up."

"Don't give it up if you don't want to," said Jake. "Let Jennifer take over running it for a while and see how it goes. You'll be only a phone call away, and we can take weekend trips to check on it. It might be fun. You can exhibit your work there and paint here."

"Okay, I like that idea, but I'm not going to clean this place and do all the laundry for the guests you plan on having," Megan complained, poking him in his chest, making her point, and laughing.

"No, we can hire someone local for that, and maybe a gardener, too. I'd want to bring back the gardens as your gran had them, with lots of flowers and places for people to sit and enjoy."

"I think I'd like that. A cozy bed and breakfast sounds wonderful. It's funny, but I've been thinking the same thing about the house. I didn't want to sell it. I love being here with you. It feels like home."

"Together, we can make anything happen," Jake said, taking Megan in his arms. He kissed her deeply, with all the love and passion he had to give. She melted into his kisses and responded intensely, drawing him into her.

Chapter 28

They sat at the kitchen table the next morning, enjoying the pancakes Jake had whipped up. Warm syrup and butter melted down the sides of the stacks.

"You remember we talked about the possibility of making the room over the garage into a studio? How about we take a look at it now? Let's see if it might work and if it needs anything major done," Megan said, warming to the idea of her own studio.

"Sure. Good idea. After we finish eating, I'll get some flashlights, in case the lights don't work over there."

About an hour later, Jake and Megan grabbed their coats and a couple of flashlights, found the keys to the garage, and crossed the yard.

The lower garage was still filled with garden equipment. There were a couple of old mowers and hedge trimmers along with garden hoses, watering cans, and some old car stuff. Bald tires and rusty paint cans added to the clutter. Cobwebs and spiders were everywhere. Megan was less than thrilled about the state the garage was in as she brushed cobwebs from her hair and spiders off her clothes. If the garage was this bad, what would the space above it be like?

"Here's yet another area that needs cleaning out!" she said. "You're going to need to be able to get your car in here this winter." Megan wondered what it would take to make the garage neat and useful again, starting with getting rid of the spiders.

"Hey, who's going to do the shoveling? We need some ground rules around here," Jake joked, holding up a worn and useless snow shovel.

"You're the rich mystery writer; hire someone!" Megan quipped back.

Jake found the trapdoor in the ceiling that led to the space above the garage and pulled on the rope, letting the steps down. He climbed up carefully while Megan waited at the bottom, holding the rickety ladder-like stairs.

"Someone's been up here," Jake called down. "Come up, but be careful."

Megan climbed slowly and soon could see in the dim light cast by the flashlight that someone had been spending a lot of time up there.

The area was bigger than they had first thought. Someone had brought up a sleeping bag, and there were empty food containers and candy wrappers scattered around. A battery-operated camping lamp was beside the makeshift bed.

"All the comforts of home," Jake said.

"This gives me the creeps," Megan said, wrapping her arms around herself and shaking at the thoughts going through her head. "Who has been camping here and since when? Maybe our intruder has been here all along."

"Well, we know now why there was never a strange car around. Our thief could walk here or get a ride and hide out until nighttime and then sneak over without being seen. "

"Okay, but how is he getting into the house? He must have gotten a key somehow."

"Or he's a very good lock-picker, but I'm betting he has keys to the house. I don't think he's in all this alone. There has to be someone helping him and feeding him information," Jake said, turning to help Megan down the stairs.

"Let's get out of here and start putting our plan in motion. I'm more than ready to get this over with," Megan said, angry now that they'd made the new discovery.

After they closed up the stairs, they walked back to the house—discussing their plan to talk to everyone about finding the necklace.

*****

Across the street, a man in jeans, a tan jacket, navy Red Sox cap, and sunglasses paused under a large oak tree still shedding its leaves. He didn't even bother to scoot behind the tree. He knew he was just one of many passersby who logged miles down this lane. He'd seen scads of them over the past month.

He watched the goings-on at Corey Bishop's house and wondered if they had found the hiding place in the space over the garage. Did they go up there, or just check out the garage? Those two snoops were a pain in the backside, and the sooner this was over, the better.

*****

Jake called Detective Yarborough to fill him in. The detective was less than enthusiastic as Jake told him about finding the necklace and discovering the hideaway over the garage.

"That certainly explains why there were never any strange cars seen in the area," the detective said, agreeing with Jake. "I'm with you in thinking that he has gotten keys to the house somehow as well. He waits up there, and he can go over anytime he wants."

Then Jake told him of his plans for Halloween night.

Yarborough blew a gasket. Megan could hear him yelling through the phone. "Are you two out of your tiny little minds? Do you think that putting Megan out there in danger is a good way to trap your intruder? Remember what he did to Zack Longstreet? He tried to cave his head in and sent him to the hospital. If what you think is true, he's killed two people already. Do you think he won't kill Megan if she gets between him and that jewelry?"

"I know the risk, and so does Megan. We want to get on with our lives, and we can't until this guy is caught and put away. If you have a better idea, I'd love to hear it, but if not, we're going ahead with this and would like your help."

"I'll help but this better work," said the detective, reluctantly.

Jake and Yarborough spent the next half hour going over what they could do to snare this guy. After discussing it, both of them were satisfied and had a plan worked out.

Jake and Megan sat at the kitchen table with their cups of coffee, continuing to talk about the risks and reservations the detective had mentioned.

"Look, if you don't want to go along with this, I'll understand, and we can try to come up with something else. There is a risk, but if we do it right, we can get this guy. Detective Yarborough and I can work on the details. You just have to be your beautiful self and wear the necklace."

"And I get to be the bait for a lunatic trying to kill me. Great," Megan moaned. "But I want to get this over with, too, and I'm willing to give it a try. I'm afraid to do this, but I'm more afraid not to."

Chapter 29

Megan called Mr. Halloran's office and spoke with Miss Parrish about setting up an appointment for later in the afternoon. She told Miss Parrish it had to do with the house, and that was all the information she shared.

The cleaners had come and were done by noon. The house was back to normal and ready for Halloween night.

Right after the cleaners left, Megan and Jake left, too. Their first stop was the Salem History Museum to see Jane.

Jane was now using Clarissa's office and had her own assistant. The assistant was a young girl named Rachael, who showed them in to see Jane.

"What a pleasure to see you! I thought you might have gone back to New York by this time, Megan. Is Salem growing on you?" Jane asked pleasantly.

"As a matter of fact, it is, and we have some surprising news," Megan glowed.

"Oh? Please, have a seat and tell me all about it."

"Where do I begin? First, we found the treasure! Can you believe it? It was in the house all along. Jake and I found it in a secret drawer in an oak trunk in the attic. The treasure is a wonderful gold-and-emerald necklace and earring set that was given as a wedding gift to one of my ancestors from her husband. We had it appraised and are going to put it in a safety deposit box."

"I'm dumbfounded," Jane said. "I didn't believe in those old rumors. I know Clarissa must have—she was doing a lot of research to find out what it might be. She had narrowed it down and knew it had to be something small. All she was finding were receipts for the sale of ships or a bit of land. She did speculate that it might be a piece of valuable jewelry. And to imagine it was in an old trunk! How on earth did you find the hidden drawer?" Jane was very curious.

"We had to unravel a bunch of riddles. Megan's gran left her a note that started it all," said Jake, not wanting to give too much away.

"Anyway, we're having a Halloween party and would love to have you come," Megan said cheerily.

"Costume is optional, but Megan and I will be dressing up. Megan is going to wear a period outfit and the family necklace and earrings. We'll put them in the bank deposit vault the next day. With all that has been going on, we feel it's not safe to keep them at the house." Jake laid the trap. Just who they would trap was the question.

"I'd love to come. I can't wait! I'll have to come up with a costume. What fun!" Jane had some ideas of her own for Halloween night.

"We'd better get going. We've got lots to do to get ready. It should be an interesting evening," said Jake.

Megan and Jake walked out to his car. He pressed the remote and opened the doors. Settling in, he started the engine and powered up the heater. "Well, what do you think?" he asked Megan.

"I'm not sure, but I don't believe it could be her. She worked for Clarissa for ages."

They decided to try and catch Mr. Prendergast next. They drove across town to his office and parked the car.

"We can tell him the same thing we told Jane," said Jake. "We have an interesting list of suspects. We better go to the Dockside after this and see if we can talk to Kathy before she goes home for the day."

"Sounds like a plan. Let's get this over with," Megan said.

They walked in and asked the receptionist if they could see Mr. Prendergast. She went to his office and reappeared quickly.

"Mr. Prendergast will see you."

"Thank you," Jake said. The young girl showed them back and returned to her desk.

"Well, well, come in, come in. Have you decided to sell that old relic of a house? You won't get a better offer—and if you do, I can beat it." Prendergast pulled out chairs in front of his desk. "Have a seat. What can I do for you?"

"We have done a lot of thinking about the house and have decided to keep it for a while," Megan said.

"The housing market is slow right now, and Megan wants to take her time," Jake said.

"I can see your point, but it's going to be a long while before the market starts to improve. How much money do you want to sink into keeping that place going?"

"We may not have to worry about that," Megan said with a smile.

"You see, we found the treasure that was rumored to be in the house. It was in an old trunk up in the attic. The treasure is a wonderful gold-and-emerald necklace and earrings set that belonged to one of Megan's ancestors. We had it appraised in Boston, and it's worth a lot of money."

"Really? I thought that was just some old wives' tale that had been running around the family. Mrs. Bishop mentioned it one time, but just as a family tale of sorts. I can't believe that you found it and that it's worth something," Prendergast said, shaking his head in disbelief.

"Anyway, we're planning a Halloween party and would like you and maybe a guest to come," Megan said. "Costumes are optional, but we hope everyone will join in the fun. I'm dressing up and wearing the jewelry that night. The next day we're putting it in the bank for safekeeping. You can't be too careful these days."

"Megan doesn't have many friends in Salem and would like to have a party in the old house before she goes back to New York," Jake said, adding another lie to the pile.

"I'd be delighted to come. I'll have to think about a guest and a costume. It's been years since I was invited to a proper Halloween costume party." Prendergast tried to remember when he had been asked to any kind of party. "That's nice of you to think of me."

They carried on a bit of small talk, and then Megan and Jake made their excuses and said they would see him at the party.

*****

Back in the car, Jake started the engine. "Last stop, the Dockside," he said. "We can grab something quick for now and order something to go for later. How's that sound?"

"Sounds good to me. I don't want to fuss tonight. You know, I hope this works. One of these people is our thief and a murderer. It's terrible, but it's true. We have just invited a killer to a Halloween party at our house. How insane is that?"

They drove along streets decked out for the upcoming Halloween evening. Most of the houses had decorations in the yards or on the porches. Quaint little shops had Halloween or fall items displayed in their window showcases. The Halloween ghost tour participants were out walking the streets. The day had been warm, but now a dry chill was in the air. The fallen leaves were scuttling along, creating a creepy, rustling sound. Everyone was getting ready for the big night.

Someone else was also preparing for the big night. Someone who was going to get what they thought was theirs by right and didn't care who got hurt along the way.

Chapter 30

Jake pulled the car into the parking lot at the Dockside. Tourist vehicles from all over New England crowded the lot. A long line of people waited on the wharf for a harbor tour on the schooner Fame.

Kathy greeted them warmly as they walked in the door. "Hi, folks! You're getting to be regulars in here. It looks like you'll be staying around for a while. I've got one booth left by the kitchen. I hope that's okay?"

"That's just fine, Kathy. It also looks like you have your hands full today." Megan smiled and followed Kathy to the booth.

"It will be over soon. In November, Salem will be almost a ghost town. Not much happens around here in the winter. It gives us locals a bit of a break," Kathy said.

Megan and Jake slid into the booth as Kathy set down some placemats and silverware for them.

"Thanks, Kathy. I know you're busy, but we have some news," Jake started to say, but Megan jumped right in.

"We found the treasure in Gran's house! It's a wonderful gold-and-emerald necklace and earrings set. We found out it was a wedding gift to one of my ancestors, and for some reason, it was put up in an old trunk in the attic. The most wonderful part is that there was the dress that the Lady in Green is wearing in her portrait."

"Megan is going to dress as the Lady in Green for Halloween and wear the jewelry. The following day it's going into the bank for safekeeping," said Jake.

"Well, I guess you two have been busy: mysterious intruders, hidden treasure, and people getting murdered! Things sure have not been dull since you got here. I can't wait for Halloween night to see what else you two can get into," Kathy said, taking her order pad out of her pocket and her pencil from behind her ear.

"I'm sure there will be a couple of surprises for our guests that night," said Megan. "We're a bit excited about the evening, too." Megan took Jake's hand in hers under the table and squeezed it.

"We won't keep you, Kathy. Can we just have two iced coffees, one BLT on toasted white bread, one chicken salad sandwich on whole wheat, and a quart of minestrone soup to go?" asked Jake. "We have a lot to do to get ready for tomorrow night."

After Kathy left, Megan nudged Jake. "Don't look now, but Julia Parrish is here with a rather scruffy-looking individual. They're in a booth near the front windows. I wonder if that's her cousin Kathy told us about."

"I think it probably is. They seem very involved in their conversation," Jake said, connecting maybe another dot.

Kathy brought back their coffee and sandwiches, saying the to-go-order would be just another minute. Jake and Megan asked her about the person who was with Julia.

"That's her cousin Frank. She and Frank have always been very close, strangely close. He's always seemed a bit slow and will do almost anything she says. I went to school with him, and he was the playground bully. Julia would use him to go after kids she didn't like. He always just gave me the creeps." Kathy buzzed off when another customer waved for her attention.

Julia looked up and saw Megan and Jake across the café. Megan saw Julia's eyes dart her way and quickly back to her conversation with her cousin. Apparently, she did not want to be noticed.

After they finished their lunch, Kathy gave them their soup to take home.

"Thanks, Kathy. We'll see you tomorrow night. I can't believe I've been here in Salem this long. The time is just flying by, and I feel so at home here," Megan said, taking the bag with their supper in it.

"I know what you mean. The older I get, the quicker it goes by. I tucked some nice fresh rolls in the bag for you as well. Enjoy, and I'll be there tomorrow night. I'll be the hobo with a red bandana sack on a stick." Kathy did a little happy dance while taking their bill to the register.

Megan and Jake finished up and were about to leave when Julia and her cousin Frank also stood to leave. There was no way either pair could avoid each other.

"Hello, Julia, nice to see you again so soon. This is a great place for lunch. Do you come here a lot?" Megan asked politely.

"It's close to the office and not too expensive, so, yes. It's one of my favorites," Julia said icily.

"Hi, I'm Jake, and this is Megan. I don't believe we've met," Jake said, extending his hand to Julia's cousin. He didn't want Julia to know he had been asking Kathy questions.

"I'm Julia's cousin, Frank," he told Jake gruffly. He reluctantly shook Jake's hand.

Jake was summing Frank up. Was he the intruder who had fired at him in the attic? He was about the right height, but Jake thought he didn't look intelligent enough to be pulling off all the murders.

"Nice bumping into you, but we have to run—so much to do before tomorrow night," said Megan as she and Jake headed out the door. "Please come, Julia—and you're invited, too, Frank, if you'd like to come. I hope Julia told you about our Halloween party. It's going to be a fun evening."

*****

Once in the car, Megan let out a deep breath of relief. "I can't believe I had the nerve to say all that—and you, too. He might be the one who shot at you and tried to kill you."

"Yeah, I know." Jake was silent for a moment as he also imagined what might have happened. Brushing away the sad thought, he continued. "We need to get going and stop by the cleaners to pick up your dress before they close.

"Is there anything else we need to do before we go home?" Jake looked over to see Megan wipe a tear from her eyes.

She saw him watching her. "I'm okay. It's just the stress of the whole thing."

"Do you want to put off the wedding for a while until things settle down and this whole thief and murder thing is solved?" he asked. He took her hand and gently kissed it.

"Oh, Jake, no, that's not it. I want to marry you tomorrow night. I'm afraid of catching this guy, and I'm afraid of not catching him tomorrow. I want to spend the rest of my life with you. I want to have all our plans for our future happen."

"They will, you'll see. After tomorrow night, I'll make all your dreams come true, I promise." Jake wiped away her tears. "Don't worry. Everything will be fine."

Megan took another deep breath. "Right, I feel better. We can do this. Just keep reminding me. Let's get my dress and go home."

*****

Fur Ball was waiting for them at the door when they got home. After untangling the cat from around her feet, Megan rushed up the stairs to put her dress away. Jake went into the kitchen to put the soup in the fridge and feed Fur Ball. He looked around for any signs that someone had been in the house while they were gone. Everything seemed to be as they left it for a change.

When Megan came down, she found him in the kitchen washing up the few dishes left from the morning.

"Hey, mister, you have any ideas on how to pass a bit of time this afternoon? I'm getting married tomorrow, and this is my last day as a single lady," she said. Megan slid her arms around his waist, started to unbuckle his belt, and worked on his zipper.

"Hey, I still have dishwater and suds all over my hands. That's not fair."

"Well, if you want to show a girl a good time, you'd better dry your hands and find something else to do with them." Megan giggled.

Jake grabbed a hand towel, dried his hands, and turned to engulf Megan in his arms. He took his time and gave her a kiss that curled her toes.

"Mmmmm, that's better," she moaned, slipping his pants below his hips.

"Oh, no, you don't!" Jake laughed and started to unbutton Megan's blouse. He stepped out of his pants as he slipped off her shirt, dropping it to the kitchen floor. He lifted her, not able to wait a moment longer than necessary, and carried her to her grandmother's old bedroom behind the kitchen.

*****

Megan woke up and stretched out her arm, feeling for Jake beside her. She felt his depression in the pillow but no Jake. Wrapping a robe around her naked body, she wandered into the kitchen. Jake was standing at the stove heating up the minestrone soup for supper.

"Hi, sleepyhead. I thought I'd let you rest a bit longer," Jake said, kissing her gently. "I've got the rolls heating in the oven. Dinner will be ready in a minute."

Megan took the bowls for the soup out of the cupboard and laid the table for their supper.

"This is nice. I want every afternoon to be exactly like this," Megan said, sitting at the table, with Fur Ball wrapping around her legs and looking for attention.

"I've been thinking about a honeymoon. What about somewhere hot and exotic?" Jake asked, ladling the steaming soup into the bowls.

"You're up to something, I can tell. You have that little tweak of mischief in your eyes. What have you done? Did you go and book a trip to Tahiti or somewhere?"

"It's definitely somewhere. Remember how you said that you always wanted to take a trip on a windjammer off the coast of Maine? Well, how about a trip on a windjammer, but from Maine to the Caribbean?"

"Jake?" Megan jumped up and hugged him so hard he thought his ribs would crack. "However, did you manage that?"

"Let's just say I know a man who knows a man. There's a schooner repositioning for the winter. She will sail out of

Camden with us aboard, and a couple weeks later, we arrive in the Caribbean. My agent was able to set it up for us through a friend of his. We have to be in Camden a week from today, or they go without us."

"Let's just hope this whole mess is settled by then," Megan said, blowing on her soup to cool it a bit.

"It will be, don't worry."

"What are we going to do with Fur Ball? We don't have anyone to watch her. Do you think Zack and Amanda would take her while we're gone?" Megan picked up the black cat and rubbed her face in the soft, shiny fur.

"It's all taken care of. I already asked Amanda, and she's happy to do it for you. I told her you needed a break from all the stress."

"I can't believe you did all this without me knowing, Jake! Thank you so much. I can't wait to go! That's one more reason why I love you so much."

"There's just one more thing. Do you think we can call this cat something besides Fur Ball? He's growing up and needs a real name if he's going to be sticking around."

"I'll try and come up with something special for him," Megan said, stroking the cat's soft black fur.

Chapter 31

The next morning was the big day. Megan and Jake were up and dressed early. They discussed new names for the kitten as they finished their coffee in the kitchen when someone knocked at the front door.

"I'll get it. It's probably the florist," she said, padding to the front door in her bare feet.

Megan was surprised to see Mr. Prendergast standing on the doorstep.

"Hi, Megan, I hope it's not too early for you. I just wanted to stop by and say I found a great smaller house a couple blocks from here. I'm willing to make a trade with you. I take this one off your hands, and you can have the smaller one, much better for a woman alone."

"She's not alone, Mr. Prendergast," Jake said, coming up behind Megan. "We appreciate the offer, but the house is not for sale or trade."

"Well, I think that's for Megan to say, Jake."

"Look, Mr. Prendergast," said Megan, "for the very last time, I am not selling the house. I love it—ghosts, burglars and all. I'm sorry, but that's it. Now, we have a lot to do before the party tonight, and I still hope you'll come. No hard feelings," Megan replied.

"No hard feelings. I just had to try one more time. Good day to you both, and I'll be coming tonight. I wouldn't want to miss the last chance to see the treasure." Prendergast said. He turned and waddled back to his car.

Megan watched him drive away and said, "That man gets on my nerves."

"He is persistent. I'll give him that," Jake said, grabbing Fur Ball, who was trying to escape out the open door. "Oh, no, you don't! I'm not looking all over the place for you today."

The florist pulled up as Jake scooped up Fur Ball. Megan strolled back to the kitchen to wash up the few dishes in the sink while Jake let the florist in.

She ordered flower arrangements for the tables in the foyer and the dining room and baskets of colorful chrysanthemums for the fireplace hearth and the bottom of the winding staircase. The place looked wonderful. Silk fall leaves, intertwined with small lights that would twinkle that evening, wound around the staircase handrail. The effect carried over to the mantelpiece in the sitting room. Later on, Megan and Jake would have their wedding ceremony there in front of the glowing fireplace.

The caterers started to bring in the plates and glasses and set them up in the dining room. In a while, they would bring in the food and drink for the guests.

Megan was getting more nervous by the minute. She was a wreck by the time the caterers finished in the dining room, but it looked perfect. The glasses would sparkle in the soft light of the candles on the table later that evening. The food waiting in the fridge looked wonderful, but she had no appetite. She wandered around the rooms just thinking about the evening to come. She was getting married in a couple of hours to a man she had just met, in front of people she had just met, and hoped a killer would come and try to take her precious necklace from her.

I must be crazy as a loon, she thought.

"Penny, for your thoughts," Jake said, coming up behind her. He put his arms around her and nuzzled her neck.

"I was just thinking how strange this all is. I'm throwing a party for a murderer on my wedding day," Megan said, leaning into Jake's caresses.

"How about a glass of wine to quiet your nerves?" Jake offered.

"How about something a bit stronger? I think there's still a bottle of Irish whiskey from the funeral in the cupboard over there."

Jack went to the cupboard and took out two whisky glasses and a half-empty bottle of Black Bush. He poured them each one and handed Megan hers.

Megan and Jake sat on the sofa with their drinks, looking at the fire dance in the fireplace. They were so comfortable with each other that words were not necessary.

Another knock at the door disturbed their musings.

Jake answered the door this time and was pleased to see Zack and Amanda. The nights were getting a bit chilly now, and Amanda wore a pretty blue wool jacket that showed off her dark hair and eyes. Zack, on the other hand, still wore his cargo shorts and leather sandals with his old canvas hat on his head.

"Hi, Jake, I hope you don't mind. We thought we'd stop over and see if you were all set for tonight," Amanda said.

"Come on in and have a drink with us. We're just relaxing in the sitting room."

"Sure, but we can't stay long. We have a few things left to do to get ready for the pre-party at our house," Zack said as he walked with Jake and Amanda toward the cozy room.

"Hi, Megan," Amanda said. She found a comfortable seat by the fire, and Zack stood behind her.

Jake poured their friends a glass of wine and topped off a bit of whiskey in Megan's and his glasses.

"All set for the party tonight?" Amanda asked.

"Definitely, you're bringing your group over here by 8:30, right?" Jake said.

"Right as rain. We just got home from the gallery. We only have a couple of finishing touches to do and get our costumes on. This is going to be such fun! I hope you like our friends. They are a good group," said Zack.

"You know what we're wearing. What are you two doing for costumes?" Jake asked the couple.

"We're not telling. I did think of going as a one-eared Van Gogh, and Amanda could be the Mona Lisa, but that's too obvious. So you will just have to wait and see!" Zack said gleefully, draining his glass. "We'd better go. Thanks for the drink. What are you two doing for Thanksgiving? We thought we might have a few friends over."

"Thanks for the invite. We'll have to let you know, but it sounds like a great plan," Megan said.

Megan walked them to the door and hugged Amanda.

"See you soon. Fingers crossed it all goes well tonight," Amanda said, hugging back.

"Better cross more than your fingers," Megan replied, worrying silently about all that might and would happen tonight.

Chapter 32

On the way back to their house, Amanda and Zack talked about the few things left to do. Zack stopped to straighten a couple of zombies on the lawn and tweak the orange lights glowing in the bushes.

Amanda asked, "What do you think she meant by 'better cross more than your fingers?' You don't think she's nervous about the party?

After all, there will be a lot of people she doesn't know there. I just get the feeling that there's something they're not telling us."

"I'm sure it's just nerves, hoping that everyone enjoys the party. What else could it be?"

"I don't know. It's just a feeling I have that there's more going on here than we know."

*****

Megan and Jake cleaned up the few glasses and put Fur Ball in an unused bedroom upstairs, out of the way. "No way are you getting into trouble tonight. We have enough to worry about," Jake said. He closed the door and hoped Fur Ball wouldn't howl the house down.

The catering servers arrived to start placing the food on trays and get the bar area stocked. Megan and Jake had about an hour to go before their guests would arrive, followed by the guests that Amanda and Zack would bring.

"Tell you what. I'll get dressed and see to the guests as they arrive, and you can take a nice bath, relax, and make a grand entrance after most of them are here. I'll send Amanda up to let you know when it's time to come down. How does that sound?" Jake asked, taking Megan in his arms.

"It's almost over. Tomorrow, no matter what, you and I will be married, and the jewelry will be in the bank. Detective Yarborough and his men are going to be here tonight. They will be in costume and mixing with the guests. Don't worry. Everything will be just fine. Go take your bath, and use some of that nice smelly bath stuff I like." Jake kissed her. He then turned her around to face the bathroom and slipped her robe off. He gave her an affectionate slap on her naked backside.

"Don't come down until Amanda comes to get you."

*****

Jake gathered his costume together and laid it out on the bed. Men in the 1800s had a lot more to put on than now. If he had been living in this house in 1850, when they thought the house had been built, he would have had a servant to help him with all the trappings and buttons.

Before donning his outfit, he stepped into the bathroom to shave and watched Megan soak in the fragrant bath for a bit.

*****

He got downstairs just as the first guests arrived. Mr. Prendergast and a friend entered when he opened the front door.

"Hello, Jake. I'd like you to meet a good friend and business associate of mine. Bob Keegan here is a local building contractor. If you plan on doing renovations to this old building, he's the best in the area."

"Welcome, and thanks for coming," said Jake, shaking their hands. "It's nice to meet you, Bob. We will be doing a lot to the place in the coming year or so. We have some big plans, and after the holidays, we'd like to get together and go over some ideas we have. Please go on in and have a drink. Make yourselves comfortable."

Next to arrive was Kathy from the Dockside Café. She had brought her boyfriend, Dave, as well. Dave made his living decoratively restoring old houses and knew Bob Keegan.

"Hey, Bob, funny meeting you here!" Dave said, extending his hand.

"You just never know who you'll bump into in Salem," Bob returned pleasantly.

Once the formalities were over, Jake went off to play host, and Dave and Bob began discussing what they might do if they were to restore Megan's house. They had worked with each other a couple times on different home makeovers in the area. Mr. Prendergast and Kathy enjoyed the exchange and occasionally offered their opinions.

While the conversation was in full swing, Amanda knocked loudly, opened the door herself, and called out, "Hope you're ready, because here we come!" She walked in with her very noisy and ready-for-fun entourage in tow.

Zack brought up the rear, ushering the last guest inside. He sported the widest grin and struck a pose beside Amanda, and asked, "Well, what do you think of our costumes?"

Jake had to laugh as he saw Zack dressed as a beekeeper and Amanda as a very sexy bee.

"Megan is going to love this!" He made some more introductions, and then Zack introduced his guests. Zack and Amanda had fifteen people with them, all dressed in a wonderful array of costumes.

This is turning out to be a great evening—or is it? Jake thought as he remembered what might happen tonight.

Last to arrive, just after Zack's group, were a couple of pirates. They milled around but didn't seem to belong to Zack's party. They kept to themselves, helping themselves to some drinks and a bit of the food. Jake saw them and made a point to go over and talk to them.

"Hello," he said. "I don't believe we've met . . ."

"Oh, yes, we have, Jake." One of the pirates lifted a mask to reveal Julia Parrish.

"Yes! Hi! That's wonderful. I'm glad you came," said Jake. "Who's your friend?"

"This is my cousin Frank. You met him at the Dockside Café. He didn't have any plans for tonight, so I brought him along, as you mentioned. I hope that's alright?"

"Sure, the more, the merrier! Please mix and mingle. Megan should be down shortly. Getting into her outfit is taking a while."

While Jake was talking to another group of guests, Julia used her cell phone and made a quick call.

Jake broke away from his conversation, deciding it was time to get Megan. He looked for Amanda to send her upstairs to see if Megan was ready.

He didn't notice that while he was looking for Amanda, someone else came in the front door and hurried up the grand staircase.

Julia and Frank noticed, however. They had been expecting that person to arrive and set their plan in motion. Julia nudged Frank, and they walked to a doorway close to the stairs.

Amanda buzzed past them at that moment, flying up the stairs to check on Megan.

Julia took a deep breath and worried that their plans would be spoiled. Amanda could complicate things a bit. They had counted on getting Megan alone somehow.

As Amanda made her way along the upstairs hallway, she heard voices coming from Megan's room. One of the voices was loud and angry.

She crept slowly toward the door to Megan's room. The door was not closed all the way, and she could see Megan seated at her dressing table. Standing across the room from Megan was a pirate erratically waving a gun—pointed at Megan.

"Your grandmother would not leave the house and let us find the treasure!" the pirate said. "We tried to scare her out, but she wouldn't go. Then she caught Frank up in the attic looking around, and when he pushed her out of the way, she fell. She would still be alive if she had just gone into a home. Old people belong in homes."

The pirate's ranting continued. "It should have been mine! He should have married my great-great-grandmother. I read it in Julia's mother's journals. She wrote down all the family history in stories. When Julia's mother died, Julia gave me the journals for the museum. I gave them to Clarissa, and she started to do the research."

"Who should have married your great-great-grandmother?" Megan asked shakily, hoping to gain some time. She was also curious to hear more about what the pirate was saying. The voice sounded vaguely familiar, but who was this woman in pirate garb?

Amanda was frozen to the spot, listening to what was happening. She pulled herself together and then dashed back downstairs to get help for Megan.

As Amanda reached the bottom step, someone grabbed her and put a hand over her mouth so she couldn't scream. She struggled against her attacker, but it was no use. They tied her up roughly, gagged her, and threw her in the coat closet under the stairs. None of the party guests saw or heard a thing. They were having a good time, and the music was playing a bit loudly.

Chapter 33

Zack, however, started to wonder where his little bee had flown off to. He found Jake and asked, "Have you seen Amanda anywhere?"

"She went up to check on Megan. I hope they're not up there just talking like girls do. We need to get this party rolling."

A gunshot rang out.

Silence filled the room and then quickly gave way to screams and loud, hurried chatter. Jake and Zack both broke into a run. They were stopped at the doorway by Julia and Frank. Jake gave Frank a hard right hook to the jaw, flattening him to the floor. Zack grappled with Julia and then tossed her aside while Jake and Zack sprinted up the stairs.

Three men dressed as eighteenth-century police took Julia and Frank into custody. Another man dressed as Sherlock Holmes darted up the stairs.

Jake and Zack burst into Megan's room to find a pirate sprawled on the floor and Megan standing with a gun pointed at the figure on the floor. Megan was shaking so badly she had to hold the gun in both hands to try and control it. "If I fire this thing, I can't be responsible for what I'll hit!" she shouted. "Please take this thing away from me. I hate guns."

As Jake took the gun carefully from Megan's hands and placed it on the bed, Zack stood over the pirate, his foot on the scoundrel's back, and looked around the room for Amanda. She was nowhere to be seen.

Jake turned back to Megan, and she dove into his arms. She started to cry and released all the tension of the last few moments in a torrent of tears.

"Don't cry, my darling," he said. "It's all over now. You're safe."

"Oh, Jake, it was awful. She was yelling about how the treasure should have been hers. She said that her great-great-grandmother should have married someone and was betrayed by my great-great-grandmother. She said stuff about Clarissa finding all this research about the two families being related. I can't remember it all right now."

"You're still shaking; you're in shock," Jake said. "How did you get the gun away from him?"

"The pirate is female; she just kept ranting, pacing around, and tripped on the rug. I grabbed the bottle of shells that Gran and I had collected and bashed her over the head. When she dropped the gun, I grabbed it, and it went off. I put a hole in the ceiling, see?" Megan sniffed and pointed up to a small hole above her head.

Zack bent over and ripped off the pirate's mask.

"Jane? You were behind all this?" Jake exclaimed. He had not suspected Jane as being part of this plot, although he had figured that Julia Parrish and her cousin Frank might be involved somehow.

"I think I can take it from here," announced Detective Yarborough, coming into the room wearing the Sherlock Holmes outfit. He took out his handcuffs and pulled Jane to her feet. She was crying, and her makeup was running down her face, making her look like a raccoon.

Zack watched Sherlock Holmes lead the pirate in handcuffs down the stairs. It wasn't until they got to the bottom that he realized it was Detective Yarborough.

He ran after him and called out, "Detective! Detective! Have you seen Amanda? I can't find her anywhere. She was supposed to be up there with Megan when we heard a gunshot. What the hell is going on?"

The detective couldn't hear Zack over the din of Jane, who screamed all the way out the door, "It should have been mine! This is all wrong. It should have been mine!" Her voice trailed away to a whimper as the detective guided her down the stairs to join her fellow conspirators.

All the guests, wondering what was going on, rushed to the doorway, but the police wouldn't let anyone go outside. They ushered everybody back into the sitting room.

Zack kept looking frantically for Amanda. She had gone to help Megan finish getting dressed, and then there was a gunshot, and now the police were not letting anyone leave the room.

"You've got to let me go!" said Zack. "My wife is missing! Has she been shot? I can't find her and don't know what's happened to her! Let me go look for her!" He spoke fast and loudly, but they simply did not pay attention to what he was saying.

Detective Yarborough walked back into the house and heard Zack pleading with the officers.

"Calm down, Zack," he said. "You know Amanda isn't in Megan's room, but maybe you should go ask her if she has seen her. You can go up now and talk to her. She might know where Amanda is."

Zack took the stairs two at a time and raced down the hall to Megan's room. He practically fell in the door. Megan was in Jake's arms softly crying, taking a deep shuddering breath now and then, and trying to pull herself together. Jake looked over at Zack and could see something was still wrong.

"What's wrong, Zack?" Jake asked, almost afraid to hear the answer.

"Amanda is missing! She was supposed to be up here helping Megan get ready, but she's not. Megan, have you seen her?"

"Zack, I'm sorry, but I didn't see her at all this evening," Megan said, her eyes widening with fear. "I was waiting for her and thought it was her coming in the room, but it was Jane Galloway, waving that infernal gun, demanding my jewelry!"

"So then, where is Amanda?" Zack asked. "She has to be here somewhere!" He was hysterical.

"We'll find her," said Jake, grabbing Zack's shoulder. "Let's you and me go downstairs and organize a search."

Jake got Detective Yarborough's okay and then told the curious guests that they had caught a thief and that the police had taken charge of her and her accomplices.

"But we have another problem," Jake said. "Amanda Longstreet is missing. We have to search the house until we find her. Please, we need everyone's help. We can start on this floor and move to the rest of the house."

Since most of the guests knew Amanda and were her friends, they were only too eager to help. Right away, they started to look in all the likely places, checking every room.

It was like a Halloween scavenger hunt, and Amanda was the prize. They scoured the backyard and porch. Gran's bedroom was searched from top to bottom. Surprisingly no one found the secret stairway to the attic, proving how well hidden it was. You had to know it was there.

Zack was passing the front stairs when he heard a banging coming from under them. The noise got louder the closer he got to the door of a small under-the-stairs closet. When he turned the knob and opened the door, he saw his Amanda tied up like a Christmas turkey. She was mad and struggling to talk with the gag still in her mouth.

Zack dove into the closet and took her in his arms, and was smothering her with kisses all over her forehead. Amanda broke his grip and smashed his chest with her hands still tied together, trying to get his attention. She then tried to yell at Zack through the gag to untie her.

"Oh, oh, right! I'm getting to that. Hold on, baby. I'll untie you."

Amanda still wanted him to take the gag off, head-butting him now in the back as he leaned over to free her feet.

He finally got the message and took the gag out of her mouth. She let out a deep breath and moved her jaw around to loosen it up before she could speak properly.

"Zack, thank goodness you found me! They just tied me up and tossed me in here. I think I broke a wing."

"Don't worry about that, as long as you're alright. I was so afraid they had killed you. I've never been so frightened in my life."

"I thought I heard a gunshot!" Amanda exclaimed. "What happened? Is Megan okay? Did anyone get hurt?"

"Everyone is fine," Zack said, helping Amanda to her feet. "Let's go call off the search and let them know you're safe. Then we can get caught up and get on with the party."

Amanda was a little roughed up. Not only was one of her wings broken, but an antenna needed to be straightened out, too. Otherwise, she was in good shape.

When Zack and Amanda walked into the sitting room, the guests there whistled and applauded, and the ones who were still out searching returned to see what the commotion was all about.

Amanda bowed and took center stage, telling what she had seen and heard upstairs and how she had been grabbed, gagged, tied up, and thrown under the stairs. Zack filled her in with what happened in Megan's room, explaining that the culprits were Jane Galloway, Julia Parrish, and Julia's cousin Frank.

Jake walked into the room and said, "If I could have your attention, please, for a minute. We have a surprise for all of you. May I present the lady of the house, the Lady in Green."

Chapter 34

All eyes turned to see Megan at the top of the stairs. She stood there just as her great-great-grandmother had so many years ago. Many gasped and started whispering about her striking appearance and resemblance to the portrait above the mantel.

When everyone quieted down, Megan started to descend the stairs.

Jake was waiting at the bottom, reaching his hand out to her. Megan had a small flash of déjá vu. She had done this before. Exactly like this before.

Dressed in the green silk dress and emeralds they had found in the attic trunk, Megan looked like a mirror image of the picture over the fireplace. Jake's breath caught, and he could hardly breathe. She was so beautiful. This time, he knew that fate had brought them together. They were traveling the road to love everlasting. Slowly she came down to meet her one true love. Jake took her hand in his, and together they walked into the room.

The fire was lit and glowing, giving the room a welcoming, relaxed feel. Bouquets of fall flowers positioned around the room softened the Halloween feel.

Throughout the room, guests were dressed for Halloween. Almost all of them wore costumes. Standing by the fireplace was a small man dressed as a cleric. Two men dressed in nineteenth-century police uniforms stood in the back of the room. Detective Yarborough had left them on duty, just in case anything else happened.

Mr. Halloran wore the wig and outfit of a London barrister. There was also the customary assortment: Cleopatras with their Marc Anthonys, witches with their warlocks, princesses with their princes, mummies, and vampires, as well as fairies here and there.

The guests made way for the couple and formed an aisle for them. Several heads continued to turn from Megan to the portrait and back again. Whispered questions floated around the room. Megan was the spitting image of the Lady in Green. She looked gorgeous. Her hair was piled on her head, just like the subject in the painting. The dress fitted like a dream, and the jewelry sparkled in the lights.

Jake and Megan walked hand in hand up to the fireplace and then turned to greet their guests.

"This night is special in so many ways," Jake said. "We want to thank you all for coming. Thank you to Zack and Amanda for all the Halloween decorations."

The guests clapped.

"We need to apologize to you two," Jake said, facing the Longstreets. "We did have an ulterior motive for having the party here tonight instead of at your house. Megan and I have been keeping a secret from you."

Jake paused, and Megan said, "You're all invited to our wedding—right here, right now, tonight. Our friend here is Mr. Purlmutter." She motioned to the man dressed as a cleric. "He's a justice of the peace and will perform the ceremony for us."

"Zack and Amanda, we would like you to be our witnesses, please. You have been beside us since the day I arrived," Megan said, putting her hand over her heart and looking at the couple.

Amanda covered her mouth with her hands in surprise and started to weep with joy. Zack just lowered his head, shaking it slowly back and forth, laughing softly in disbelief.

"After the ceremony, Megan and I will tell you the tale of the lost treasure of the Claddagh ring," Jake announced mysteriously. Then he turned back to the cleric and politely said, "We're ready."

Mr. Purlmutter began the formalities, saying, "Ladies and gentlemen, we are gathered here today to witness the joining of these two people in the bonds of matrimony." He continued with the ceremony and called for Jake and Megan to say their vows and exchange rings.

Megan slipped the gold Claddagh ring they had bought in Boston onto Jake's finger, and she spoke her vows.

"Jake, the fates have brought us together, and our love for each other has endured. I promise to love you always and support your dreams as my own. Together we can face whatever lies ahead. I hope to bring you happiness and comfort for the rest of our lives." Megan wiped a tear of joy from her eye, her smile lighting her face with love for Jake.

"Megan, from the moment I saw you, I knew we would spend our lives together. I didn't realize there would be so much excitement, but it bonded us to each other and made us stronger. We make a good team, and that is what a marriage is. I love you with all my heart and promise to honor and protect you for the rest of my life."

After Jake finished speaking, he placed the gold and emerald ring that had been her great-great grandmother's on her hand and took a deep breath to release the tension he had been holding inside.

Amanda was still blubbering, and a few more of the women also were moved to tears.

Mr. Purlmutter announced, "I now pronounce you man and wife. You may kiss your bride."

Jake took Megan in his arms and kissed her, a long and loving kiss that held the guests spellbound.

"Ladies and gentlemen, may I present Mr. and Mrs. Jackson Durant," Mr. Purlmutter said, and the ceremony was officially over.

The gathering erupted with more applause and cheers. Jake shook hands with the justice of the peace, handed him an envelope containing his fee, and thanked him for his services.

Megan hugged Amanda, who had finally stopped crying. Zack went up to Jake and punched him in the shoulder. "What a way to keep a secret. You know how to throw a party—cops, gunshots, burglars, not to mention my wife tied up in a closet! And then you top it off with a surprise wedding! This party is going to be the talk of Salem. Did I mention finding a one-hundred-and-fifty-year-old treasure and your wife looking like her dead ancestor? Living next to you is going to be fun, I can tell."

"I can assure you it's not going to be like that. We just want to live a quiet life and open a guest house. Megan can have her art studio, and I can write a few more best sellers. We are going to be your normal, married couple."

More guests came up to congratulate the pair. Several asked about the tale he had promised.

"Ah, yes: the tale of the lost treasure of the Claddagh ring. Please, pour a drink, grab a bite to eat, get comfortable, and we shall begin." Jake said dramatically, trying to sound all deep and mysterious.

Chapter 35

"The story began in 1850. A wealthy man, Laurence Sinclair, met the beautiful Lucinda Corey. He built this big house for her and planned to fill the bedrooms with the children they would have. As a bridal gift for the lovely Lucinda, he bought the jewelry that Megan is wearing tonight. He gave it to her to wear at their wedding. On their first anniversary, Lucinda gave him a portrait of herself—the painting of the Lady in Green you see over the mantel. She also told him the news that she was pregnant." Jake stopped to take a sip of his drink. Megan continued the story.

"Unfortunately—as happened a lot in those days—Lucinda went into labor and had a very hard time of it. She delivered a baby girl—a healthy, adorable, pink bundle of joy. Lucinda and Laurence were thrilled. The baby flourished, and they named her Mary Louise Corey Sinclair. As much as the baby thrived and grew, Lucinda's health declined."

"Shortly after Mary Louise turned three, Lucinda died," said Jake. "Laurence was devastated."

"He took her green silk wedding dress and the gold and emeralds he had given her and hid them away in a trunk in the attic," said Megan. "My thought is he couldn't bear to look at them because of the grief in his heart. He planned to tell Mary Louise about them when she was old enough."

"Unfortunately, again tragedy struck, and Laurence lost his life in a hunting accident," Jake said. "Not from a gunshot, as you might expect. No. He broke his neck fox hunting. His horse shied at the last minute, and he fell."

"The treasure was lost," Megan said. "Rumors traveled through the family about it and where it might be. Clues leading to the location had been left, maybe by Laurence or someone close to him, at the time of his death. As the months and years went on, even the clues were lost, until now."

Megan held up her left hand. "My grandmother left me the Claddagh ring after her death," she said. "Pieces of the puzzle started to fall into place. The portrait of the Lady in Green turned up in the Longstreet Gallery. It freaked me out when I saw it. Yet it provided us with another piece to the puzzle."

Megan's eyes grew misty. "Unbeknownst to us, all this time, another person was also after the treasure," she said. "They were so obsessed with finding it; they killed whoever got in their way— including my grandmother and Clarissa McDowell." Megan felt a tear or two run down her cheeks.

Everyone gasped and started talking.

Jake clinked his glass with his ring to get everyone's attention. As soon as they quieted and Megan composed herself, she said, "They would have killed me tonight to get the treasure, except Jane tripped over a wrinkled rug. I grabbed the jar of shells Gran and I had collected all those years ago and bashed her over the head. Through all of this,

I was helped by Lucinda and her love for Laurence. Now that the treasure has been found, I feel they're at peace at last."

*****

The room buzzed with conversations about the treasure and the evening's unexpected twists and turns. Guests congratulated the happy couple and expressed their happiness that murder had been thwarted this time. And then, around eleven o'clock, the guests started to depart and find their way home.

Zack and Amanda stayed to help clean up after the party. The caterers would come back in the morning to collect their trays and other serving utensils.

The doorbell rang right at midnight.

"At midnight on Halloween? Who could that be?" Megan asked.

"Don't open it," Zack whispered. "It could be a ghost or a zombie."

"For Pete's sakes, Zack, get a grip," Amanda said, walking to the big front door. "There are no such things."

She opened the door slowly just the same, to be on the safe side.

Chapter 36

"Hello, Amanda," Detective Yarborough said as he stepped inside. "I hope it's not too late. I've just come from questioning Jane and her accomplices. I thought you would all like to know what I found out."

Coming in from the kitchen, Jake was wiping his wet hands on a towel. He had finished washing up the last of the glasses.

"Please come in, Detective. Can I offer you a drink, or are you still on duty?"

"I'm off duty and would love a scotch if you have one."

"Sorry, no Scotch. How about a drop of Irish whiskey instead?"

"That's good, too."

Once settled with a drink in his hand, Detective Yarborough told them what he had learned from talking with Jane, Julia, and Frank.

"I think this all started with some journals that Julia found after her mother passed away a few months ago," he said. "Julia's mother had written a sort of family history. Some of which I'm sure was fiction, but Julia took it as fact. It would have made a great book if it had been published."

Yarborough paused to catch his breath and take a sip of the whiskey. "Julia went to Jane to collaborate the facts she had gotten from the journals. It turns out that Jane and Julia are cousins.

"According to the journals, one of Jane's ancestors worked as a clerk in a chandler's shop down on the wharf, where Laurence Sinclair did a lot of business. She had her eye set on Laurence Sinclair, but one day, Lucinda came in and stole him away from her. This is where Jane got the idea that the treasure should have been hers. If Lucinda had not entered the picture, her ancestor probably would have married Laurence Sinclair.

"Jane was not a good researcher," Yarborough continued, "so she asked Clarissa for help. Clarissa found a reference to a 'gift of great value,' some kind of treasure, given to an ancestor, but there was no mention of it turning up in later years. The treasure, whatever it was, appeared to have been lost.

"Frank, another cousin, was brought in to search Corey Bishop's house since that house was Laurence and Lucinda's original home and had never left the family. Jane talked Julia and Frank into becoming partners in her scheme to find the treasure."

"So, just what part in all this did Julia play?" Megan asked.

"Jane got Julia to get an extra key made for the house," the detective said. "She was going to cut her cousins in on whatever they found. Your grandmother trusted everybody, so when Julia suggested that, for her safety, she should leave a key to the house with Mr. Halloran, she didn't see a problem."

"So that's why there were no signs of breaking and entering," Jake said, seeing the logic in having a key made.

Amanda edged closer to the edge of her chair and asked, "So who murdered who?"

"Frank killed your grandmother, Megan. I'm sorry I didn't see it sooner," Detective Yarborough said. "She found him searching the attic, and he pushed her down the stairs when she tried to get away. Frank was also the one who knocked you on the head, Zack."

"It still hurts when I touch that spot," Zack said, rubbing his bald, bruised head.

"So don't touch it," Amanda joked.

"Who killed Clarissa?" Jake wanted to know.

"Jane did. She found out that Julia had diabetes and took one of her syringes and filled it with air. Air injected into the bloodstream causes an air embolism and looks like a heart attack. Clarissa was starting to put two and two together about what had happened to your grandmother, Megan, and Jane couldn't have her finding out the truth."

"But Jane was so distraught when we found Clarissa dead in the office," Megan said. "I find it hard to believe that she actually killed her and then fooled us so completely."

Jake got up and walked over to stand behind Megan. He put a comforting hand on her shoulder.

"I agree she was very convincing," said Yarborough. "I found out she had some acting experience in high school and college. She even did a bit of amateur stuff in the playhouses in the area. I also think that Jane was short a few marbles toward the end. She was still ranting about being cheated.

"At the station tonight, Julia and Frank gave up Jane as the mastermind that had come up with the whole plan: It was her idea to search the house, make the key, kill Clarissa, and try to kill you tonight.

"Frank's murder of your grandmother was unfortunate. If she hadn't gone up the stairs, she would probably still be alive. If Zack had not been at the gallery, Frank would not have bashed his head in. Jane used them and fooled the rest of us."

"Thanks for coming and letting us know all this," Megan said, shaking, holding her husband's hand that rested on her shoulder for support.

The detective stood up and prepared to leave. "I hope that things will settle down here now, and you can get on with your new life in Salem. I hear congratulations are in order for your wedding."

Jake took Yarborough's empty glass, set it on the side table, and walked him to the door.

"Thanks again, Detective."

"No problem. This case was certainly a strange one."

Jake closed the door, muttering to himself, "You don't know how strange."

*****

Rejoining the others, Jake took a seat next to Megan. Magic found a soft spot in Megan's lap and was purring away. He wondered how the cat had gotten out of the upstairs bedroom but said nothing.

"Boy, when you guys throw a party, you throw a party!" Zack said, standing in front of the fireplace. "I can't wait till next year."

"Tell me about your getting married tonight," said Amanda. "Was that for real or part of the show? I still can't believe you two planned that tonight and kept it a secret." Hundreds of questions whizzed around in Amanda's head.

"We just felt it was right to get married tonight," Megan said. "Laurence and Lucinda were so much in love, just like us. We had already decided on the wedding and wanted to surprise everyone."

"You managed that just fine," said Zack. "What about the attempt on your life? Did you plan that, too?"

"Well, yes, we kind of did," Jake replied. "We had to do something to draw out whoever was causing all this trouble. I guess it worked."

"Okay, so now what? Are you going on a honeymoon now or waiting?" Amanda was still asking questions.

"If you can still watch Fur Ball excuse me, Magic for us—we found a new name for him—we would like to leave in a couple of days. We have a schooner waiting in Camden headed for the Caribbean."

"Oh, that sounds so romantic!" Amanda gushed.

"Don't get any ideas," Zack said jokingly.

"Well, thanks for an exciting evening," Amanda said as she stood up to leave. "We'd better head home and let the newlyweds have some peace and quiet for a change. Let us know what you want us to do for Magic."

"Good night to you, too, Magic," Zack said. "If you're a good kitty, I'll get you some catnip." He leaned down to stroke the cat's soft black fur.

The little cat looked up at him and, cocking his head, winked one of his amazing emerald-green eyes.

"Did you see that? She winked at me! She did—I saw it. I didn't know cats could wink!"

Amanda grabbed Zack's arm and tried to pull him toward the front door to leave. "Come on, you. Cats don't wink at people."

"Amanda, she did! She knows I'm getting her catnip." He looked over his shoulder and saw Magic wink again.

"There . . . she did it again."

Megan and Jake laughed at Zack as he protested to Amanda. She finally had Zack headed in the direction of the door. As the door closed, Megan and Jake could still hear, "But,

Amanda, he did wink at me! There's something strange about that kitten, isn't there?"

*****

Jake took Megan's hand and kissed her palm. Drawing her to him, he said, "Mrs. Durant, are you ready for bed now?"

"Yes, Mr. Durant, I believe I am."

They walked to the stairs hand in hand. They turned and took one last look at the sitting room. There they saw Laurence and Lucinda standing in front of the fireplace, holding hands and looking adoringly into each other's eyes. After just a moment, the image faded away.

"Did I just see . . .," murmured Jake.

"Naw, we couldn't have," said Megan, shaking her head. She couldn't resist a second look back over her shoulder.

The newlyweds continued up the stairs. On the landing, they passed a smiling Clarissa, dressed in a flamboyant gypsy costume, and, beside her, Corey Elizabeth Bishop, dabbing a handkerchief to her eyes, crying with joy for her granddaughter and the wonderful man with whom she would share the rest of her life.

BOOKS BY BRENDA M. SPALDING

It's 1938; the carnival is in town, and a hurricane is on the way. Driving rain and floods create havoc in the small community as the hurricane races closer.

The winds howl, and cultures clash when Michael Flannigan falls for a beautiful Russian fortune teller, Dania.

The oldest child in a strong Irish family, Michael must prove himself to his family and Dania's stubborn father, Boris Koslov.

Local lad, Johnny Russo, is found dead in Silver Lake, and the police suspect someone from the carnival is involved. The killer is on the run. Will he escape both the police and the forces of nature?

The carnival will move on, but the 'The Lake' area of Newton, Massachusetts, will be changed forever.

Megan and Josh are on a two-week vacation in Florida from Atlanta. Coming back from a day trip exploring the antique shops in Arcadia, a cow on the road puts them in a ditch on a rural back road. A miscommunication over cell phones has them stranded.   They find their way to a farmhouse, and an old woman willing to rescue and take them in until help can arrive.

Mrs. Sullivan entertains her guest with the story of how she came to live at Honey Tree Farm. She recounts meeting Jesse, the love of her life, and how a jealous bully tried to destroy their life together.

What the reader discovers is that love is precious and can indeed last beyond a lifetime.

Brenda M Spalding

Broken Branches

Brenda M Spalding

Broken Branches

Brenda M Spalding

Broken Branches

Brenda M Spalding

Broken Branches

Brenda M Spalding

Made in the USA
Columbia, SC
22 May 2021

37699702R00124